WEIRD HORROR MAGAZINE

FALL 2025

ISSUE 11

Edited by

MICHAEL KELLY

UNDERTOW
PUBLICATIONS

WEIRD HORROR 11
Fall 2025

PUBLISHER
Undertow Publications

EDITOR/LAYOUT
Michael Kelly

PROOFREADER
Carolyn Macdonell

OPINION
Simon Strantzas

COMMENTARY
Orrin Grey

COVER ART
Valin Mattheis

COVER DESIGN
Vince Haig

Weirdhorrormagazine.com

Contents

Note From the Editor   5

ON HORROR   7
Simon Strantzas

GREY'S GROTESQUERIES   11
Orrin Grey

THE START OF SOMETHING   15
David Demchuk

INVASIVE SPECIES   23
Mary Kuryla

A CRUELTY   37
Rory Say

ANOTHER MOTHER AGAIN   51
Cyan Katz

WINE-DARK EYES   61
Juniper White

WE DWELL IN ITS MANY-CHAMBERED
HEART   65
A.C. Wise

DARK WATER   75
Andrew Humphrey

FOREWORD TO 'OCCULT METHODS OF
INVESTIGATION'   91
David Peak

THE GOD OF RUST   105
Jocelyn Szczepaniak-Gillece

WE DIDN'T USED TO BE LIKE THIS   115
Jack Klausner

Contributors   130

Note From the Editor

DEAR READERS, thank you for helping us get to issue 11 of *Weird Horror* magazine. We wouldn't have made it this far without your support, and we are grateful you are on this journey with us.

You will notice two rather significant changes to this issue. Gone are the interior illustrations and also Lysette Stevenson's column, *The Macabre Reader*. It is, of course, a sad development.

Simply, I needed to cut some costs. The magazine has always faced financial challenges, but we hope this will help us continue to bring you great weird fiction.

I want to thank all the artists who have contributed to the magazine, and I especially want to thank Lysette Stevenson for 80 —80!—amazing reviews over 10 issues.

—Michael Kelly

On Horror

Simon Strantzas

The Four Quadrants

THERE ARE four types of horror story: the supernatural, the non-supernatural, the literary, and the entertaining. And there are no others.

(Just go with me on this.)

Every story falls somewhere in the quadrants formed by these two sets of extremes, and just where in the quadrants a story falls will likely dictate how much interest you, as a reader, have in it. Perhaps you like campy gory stories, or instead you like deeply-felt metaphorical stories. Or maybe both. By way of these four quadrants, Horror has you covered.

I have often claimed I prefer supernatural horror almost exclusively. There is something about a world that deviates from our own that interests me more than reality's everyday human horrors. I don't need to spend my time reading about killers and thieves and people cutting one another to shreds. It doesn't appeal to me, and the violence one often finds in these stories—the violence that separates them from thrillers, for example—is not something I want to spend too much time immersed in. The more violent it gets, the more bored I become.

Nicolas Pesce's 2016 film, "The Eyes of My Mother," was a hit within the circles I travel, and it was often recommended to me on social media. "It's right up your alley," they all told me, perhaps because of its sombre tone and striking black-and-white visuals. And while, yes, the film had plenty of both of these things, I did not find it right up my alley. Far from it, actually. Despite its beautiful compositions and interestingly perverse ideas, overall the whole film did nothing to pique my interest. The only horror it offered me was the mundane reality of a tortured life. And watching someone put through that sort of ringer—let alone feeling that I, too, was being put through that very same ringer—is just not my idea of fun.

Had its horrors been supernatural, though, I probably would have loved it. I much prefer the monster to the havoc it wreaks.

Having said all that, I experienced an epiphany recently regarding my overly-slavish devotion to all things supernatural. A colleague of mine asked if my stance excluded the fiction of Shirley Jackson, whose stories like "The Lottery" and "The Summer People" are embraced as horror despite lacking the supernatural. This simple question set off a chain reaction in my thoughts as I tried to juggle and justify my feelings about how these favourite stories (and favourite stories like them) fit into my admittedly simplistic four-quadrant organization of horror.

When I reviewed my categorization, I came to realize I'd been underestimating *literary non-supernatural* horror. I'd been thinking of it only containing thoughtful mediations on multiple murderers, child killers, and their ilk—cases where the irrationality of extreme violence exists, albeit in a less overt form. In truth, these human horrors may actually be in the minority in this quadrant, hewing closer perhaps to *entertainingly non-supernatural*. In fact, the bulk of the *literary non-supernatural* quadrant may be populated by something we might call "apparent horror," and may wholly differ not only from my misconceptions but from the other horror quadrants as well.

The first two quadrants, the *entertainingly supernatural* and the *literary supernatural*, are fairly easy to qualify as horror. The supernatural is, by definition, the invasion of the irrational into our rational world. The mere existence of the irrational is itself a horrific notion, regardless of how malignant or benign it might be. And while not every *entertainingly non-supernatural* story is a horror story, when one is, it's very easy to discern because in these stories it's the inherent violence of existence that proves to be irrational. Acts of extreme violence and depravity are so alien to our day-to-day lives that they are antithetical to our understanding of the world. And where these acts are so much less extreme that they no longer appear irrational, we find the stories move toward the tropes of Horror's sister genres like Thriller or Mystery. But *literary non-supernatural* stories are different—they may lack the irrational altogether. Or rather, the irrational is so degraded that the line between it and the rational is negligible. Instead, these sorts of stories exist in a liminal world of rationalities where things are "not quite right." Slightly askew, their axes tilted, they are stories where the everyday is corrupted just enough that the strange can leak through. In today's parlance, we might even call these stories Weird Fiction.

Because Weird Fiction can be many things, and because it lacks the boundaries of horror—or rather because those boundaries have bled into other genres—it's able to achieve some of the nuances we don't necessarily permit in Horror. The Weird is allowed to tell stories that approach Horror without ever crossing over completely. It gets close, though; perhaps closer than it does to those other genres it shares blurred space with. Because unlike science fiction or fantasy, horror is not bound by the trappings of the genre. Instead, it can get by on atmosphere. A horror story can *appear to be* a horror story, even without any of the tropes that indicate it belongs. We don't get many stories that *feel* like science fiction without something scientific, nor do we get many stories that *feel* like fantasy without the fantastic. But with horror, simply telling a story through horror's lens is enough. It's for this reason non-supernatural fiction, the kind that foregoes human horrors, can still find a place under the genre's broad umbrella.

What this all adds up to, I'm not sure I know, but I do find it interesting to consider how much time I've spent in the past arguing that the only horror fiction I preferred was supernatural-based. While I still believe this sort of story appeals to me most consistently, I must admit the stories I find most exciting at the moment are those that lean toward the *literary non-supernatural* I've outlined above. If the key to good horror is juxtaposition, then the existence of horror tales that are *not quite* horror tales is arguably the greatest juxtaposition in the field, and one that I think deserves more consideration. If not in the scope of the tales it tells, then in its connection to the other types of horror that surround it.

Grey's Grotesqueries

Orrin Grey

Monsters and Madmen: Tokusatsu Terror and the History of Monster Movies

ARE GODZILLA MOVIES HORROR?

Pondering that question is what initially kicked off this install-ment of *Grey's Grotesqueries*. Certainly, Godzilla movies are *monster* movies, and while monster movies are often considered a subset of horror, they are sometimes seen as distinct. Writing in his 1989 book *Horror Movies*, Tom Powers described the relationship thusly: "In monster movies, beasts come from faraway places. They come from exotic lands, from outer space, or from under the sea. In horror movies, on the other hand, the beasts come from within people."

This is almost certainly an oversimplification, however, not to mention one that begs more questions than it answers. After all, it seems undeniable that *Alien* is a horror movie, despite its beast that comes from "exotic lands, from outer space, or from under the sea" —although, I guess *technically* the xenomorph in *Alien* also comes "from within people." At the same time, it's hard to argue that, say, *King Kong Escapes* is a horror movie, even while it is undeniably a monster movie.

"Monster movie" as a generic descriptor isn't one that we use much these days, but it was fairly common parlance even up to the time when Tom Powers' book was being published. This was thanks in part to the "monster kid" renaissance of the 1960s, which capitalized on theatrical reissues and syndicated TV showings of classic monster films to drum up a new generation of monster movie fans.

"A monster kid is anybody who grew up reading *Famous Monsters of Filmland*," claims one person on an internet forum, in answer to the question "what is a monster kid?" Given that *Famous Monsters of Filmland* ran from 1958 until 1983, that gives us a pretty good window into when such a distinction might have been drawn—and it's probably no coincidence that most Godzilla movies came out during that period.

In their native Japan, Godzilla movies are part of a tradition called tokusatsu (literally "special filming") that describes movies or TV shows that rely heavily on special effects. While all Japanese kaiju films are tokusatsu, however, not all tokusatsu are kaiju films. Other examples of the tradition include various popular Super Sentai-type shows, which were imported and westernized to make the *Mighty Morphin' Power Rangers*, but while the form is most inextricably associated with such instances of science fiction and fantasy, tokusatsu also includes war and disaster films.

There are also many tokusatsu horror movies, several of them overseen by Godzilla's first and most prolific director, Ishiro Honda. I've written in a previous installment of this column about my affection for *Matango*, Honda's 1963 adaptation of William Hope Hodgson's seminal fungal horror story, "The Voice in the Night," but he also helmed other tokusatsu terrors including *The H-Man* (1958) and *The Human Vapor* (1960). (In all three of those cases, arguments could be made for the monsters coming both from within people *and* from outside.)

A few of the Godzilla movies themselves seem undeniably like horror, as well. The "Tokyo in flames" of the first film, with its stark images reminiscent of the devastation of the atom bomb attacks on Hiroshima and Nagasaki, certainly qualifies.

Even those films featuring the big G (and friends) that aren't quite so horrific throughout sometimes have moments of chilling or haunting weirdness. The beginning of Toho's first color kaiju feature, *Rodan*, in which a mining village encounters giant insects is a premium example of weird horror, as is a giant octopus attack early on in *War of the Gargantuas*. Even the island sequences with the giant mantises in *Son of Godzilla* are, at times, effectively creepy.

Americans got involved, too, and not just by re-editing Japanese imports to include Raymond Burr. American actors featured in several Godzilla movies, partly to increase their salability on the international market, and there were a number of American/Japanese co-productions, such as the *The Manster* (1959), a variation on the Jekyll and Hyde tale in which an American news correspondent is experimented on by a Japanese scientist and subsequently grows a second head that—as these things are wont to do—compels him to kill.

The Manster has a rather notorious reputation as a turkey but it is, for my money, a surprisingly good bit of weird horror with some absolutely unforgettable B-movie imagery, especially in its final reel, as our protagonist's dual sides split apart into separate entities and grapple on the rim of a volcano. It is also notable for having directly inspired Sam Raimi's work on a segment of *Army of Darkness*—you'll know the one once you've seen the movie.

One of the genuinely weirdest bits of Japanese/American cross-pollination in these early tokusatsu flicks is also one that I think is among the most forgotten. The American release of *Godzilla Raids Again*—the name changed to *Gigantis, the Fire Monster* —was re-dubbed, re-edited, and otherwise variously mangled, including adding in significant quantities of stock footage.

Among these are stop motion dinosaur sequences taken, at least in part, from the 1948 film *Unknown Island*, including a brief shot of a lumpy dinosaur head that looks almost exactly like an early precursor of the *Eraserhead* baby. This indelible (if brief) moment of weird horror was what I remembered most vividly about the flick from my first time watching it—so, imagine my surprise when I put on the original Japanese version and it was nowhere to be found!

America doesn't have a specific tokusatsu tradition of its own, though there are certainly plenty of American movies that would qualify if we did. Hollywood history *does* include several distinct monster movie booms, however, beginning with the Universal monsters of the 1930s.

This was followed by the "big bug" movies of the 1950s, which are mostly associated with flicks about giant, atomically mutated insects, following the success of the giant ant classic *Them!* Alongside these mutated bugs were also plenty of alien invaders, and even Godzilla himself probably wouldn't exist without theatrical re-releases of *King Kong* and the American film *The Beast from 20,000 Fathoms*.

Though often defined by relatively inexpensive slasher films, the special effects techniques and technology of the 1980s gave rise to its own wave of monster movies, often paying homage to or remaking 1950s classics, as in John Carpenter's *The Thing*, David Cronenberg's *The Fly*, and Chuck Russell's *The Blob*, to name a few.

Perhaps the best way to understand the relationship between horror and monster movies—despite Tom Powers' asserted distinction—is to imagine them as two circles of a Venn diagram which overlap more often than they don't. It is possible, of course, to have a horror film without a monster; many films do. And it's equally possible, though less common, to have a monster movie that isn't horror. Deciding which is which, however, is probably a matter of needlessly splitting hairs.

The Start of Something

David Demchuk

THIS PAST SUNDAY, around 10 a.m., as I was stepping out of the bathroom in my towel and slippers, a fluff of steam billowing around me in the chilly hallway, I saw myself standing down on the landing outside the door to the spare room, just standing and staring back at me with a faintly secretive smile. He was wearing— I was wearing—my old green plaid shirt, my faded black pants that were a bit baggy around the rear, and the dark green socks that I'd last seen gnarled up in a ball in the bin at the back of the closet. I thought to myself, I remember it clearly: *I wonder if this is the start of something.*

I don't know why I didn't call out to him—to me. I don't know why I didn't go up and say something, do something. I was startled, maybe I was afraid. Maybe I was afraid that one of us wouldn't be there when I reached him, when I reached me. Instead I turned and walked into my bedroom, hastily pulled on my dull green pants, my navy socks, my green long-sleeved thermal and my red plaid over-shirt, then steeled myself as I stepped into the hall, ready for a confrontation. I looked left and right. No sign of me. But Brian was there in his boxers, brushing his teeth, looking at me quizzically.

"I thought you were downstairs," he said, his mouth mushing around the brush and spattering flecks of foam.

15

"Were you just over by the spare room?" I asked. He shook his head. A thump from below, and then the slam of the front door. We looked at each other. He hurried back into the bathroom to spit and pull on his things while I rushed down the stairs, threw open the inside and outside doors, looked up and down the street. No one, except for a puzzled city worker sweeping garbage off the sidewalk.

"Wasn't that just you?" he asked.

"I don't know," I replied, then stepped back into the entryway and closed the door behind me. I looked down. My old running shoes were gone. Dingy white canvas, blue trim, a split down the side of the left shoe. I had so many old things scattered around the house, things I no longer wore, things I'd been meaning to get rid of. Somehow the other me had known to take them.

"What's happening?" Brian said as he stumbled down the stairs, still buttoning his shirt. I always told him not to come down in his sock feet, the steps were too slippery. "Who was that? Did someone break in?"

"I think so, yes," I answered because what else could I say. "I don't think he took anything."

"How'd he get in?" he asked, his annoyance increasing. "Wasn't the door locked?"

"I'm sure it was," I said. "You were the last one in, you always lock the door."

"Don't try to lay this on me," he warned.

"I'm just saying the door was locked," I answered, now on the verge of losing my temper. We were both stressed and upset, how could we not be? I pushed past him and headed into the kitchen.

"Where are you going?" he demanded. He doesn't like starting an argument without finishing it, and winning.

"The wallets," I said. "The wallets, the keys, the phones, the passports." This snapped him out of his temper, his eyes went wide and he ran in after me. He started picking up and flipping through random piles of papers and junk on the kitchen counter. Nothing important was there. How could he not know where everything was?

I reached across the table, grabbed our phones and wallets and keys and placed them in front of him. "Here, check through these." I pulled open the drawer that had our passports and gift cards, a few coupons, some takeout menus and old Christmas cards. Both passports were there, everything was there, except for one expired credit card that I hadn't gotten around to cutting up and throwing away. But that wouldn't be good for anything, would it? You couldn't actually use it for anything.

"It's all here," he sighed. "ID, cards, cash, all the keys. It's all good, he didn't get anything. We must have scared him off." He pulled me close and surprised me with a kiss on the forehead. "I'll have to check the door before we go to bed. I used to, didn't I?"

"Maybe we should get the locks changed, just in case." I tried to remember if I had a spare key, if I'd had one in the desk upstairs. The thought of someone who looked like me, dressed like me, coming in and out of our house without our knowing. A knot tightened in the pit of my stomach, the size of a baby's fist.

"You're right," he said. "We should do that. I can't remember if we changed them when we moved in. We must've, right?"

My phone rang, scaring us both. Unknown number. He looked at me, one of those looks that asks a question without asking a question. "I'm sure it's just spam," I said. "It can go to voicemail." I waited, we both waited. No message, just a click.

~

THE NEXT MORNING, I was coming back through the park and down to the sidewalk across from our house when Mrs. Collins from around the corner stomped up towards me and stood in front of me, furious.

"Just what do you think you're doing?" she shouted. "Have you lost your mind?" I could see past her to where a cluster of local mothers and some curious strangers were in the middle of the road. Cars were stopped, and a siren cried forlornly in the distance. Mrs. Erickson from three doors over was on her way up to join us, clutching her heavy tweed coat around herself as one of the buttons was missing.

"I have no idea what you're talking about, I'd like to get these things inside." I went to move past her but she put her hand on my shoulder and pushed me back into place.

"You wait right there until the police arrive," she said. "I'm sure they'll want to have a little chat with you."

"About what, Mrs. Collins?" The siren wove its way closer through the tangle of one-way streets and side roads. All I could think about were the eggs in the left-hand bag which the girl at the store placed too close to the top even though I warned her.

"You took that child's dog, the one from number 47—now I admit that it is a noisy dog, it whines and barks at all hours, they leave it outside far too long, but that's not the dog's fault—and it's certainly no reason to pick it up by the scruff of the neck and throw it into the middle of the street. Into traffic!" Mrs. Erickson was now standing shoulder to shoulder with her, creating a wall of middle-aged flesh between me and the house.

I knew the dog in question, and I hated the dog in question, but that was hardly the point. "What the hell are you talking about?" I asked. "When did all this happen?"

"Not ten minutes ago," she exclaimed, pointing down to the crowd on the street. "We all saw it, everyone saw it!"

"Look at me, Mrs. Collins. Look closely. Where do you think I was ten minutes ago?" I held the shopping bags up in front of her face, gave them a shake. "How would I be able to pick up a dog and throw it into the street, then magically appear at the supermarket, load a cart with a hundred dollars' worth of groceries, get someone to ring them through for me since the self-check never works, then stuff them into these ridiculous bags and walk down to this very spot, all in ten minutes?"

"Oh, well, I don't know, I—"

"What was this person wearing, this person who looked like me? Was he wearing these clothes?" I did an angry little pirouette, twirling round to glare at her. She looked me up and down, her face furrowing and reddening.

"Well, no, you—he—had a plaid shirt of some kind—"

"Exactly. It was not me, and it never would be me because I would never do such a thing." The sirens abruptly stopped just below my line of sight, red and blue lights dancing across the fronts of the houses.

"But he looked just like you."

"And you look just like John Wayne Gacy, but I don't run around calling you a murderous clown." I turned to Mrs. Erickson who had stood silent throughout, her expression changing with every twist and turn in the tale. "And what about you? Do you have something to say?"

"I never did like that dog," Mrs. Erickson confided. "If you hadn't done it—you or whoever—I might very well have done it myself."

"Well that's a comfort," I replied. "Now if you'll excuse me," and I hoisted up the shopping bags with what energy I could muster, strode across the street and through the front door, then slammed it shut behind me. It was only later, when I was unpacking the bags on the counter, the carton of eggs in my hand, that I realized the door had been unlocked. I was sure I had locked it before I left, and Brian had been gone for hours.

"Hello?" I called out to the living room, the stairwell, the floors above. The house was as still and silent as if it was holding its breath.

~

WORK WAS QUIET, maybe too quiet. No meetings, no calls, no new emails, no answers to my chats. That was fine by me, I was happy to spend some time getting things done around the house. It was well after lunch when I was cleaning the bathroom that I heard some kind of hubbub out front, like someone was having a fight. *What now?* I swung open the shutters and looked out onto the street. Down the road at the Erickson house, a window on the top floor was open to the warm afternoon air, and Mrs. Erickson was leaning out across the sill holding a squirming screaming baby over the sidewalk below. Her grandchild, presumably. Then a shriek and a scuffle, and another Mrs. Erickson reached out and grabbed the first by the hair, pulling her and the baby inside. Down below, the garbage sweeper from the previous day ran along the street and through the intersection, chasing a municipal maintenance truck that he was also driving.

I couldn't let myself think about what any of this meant. I closed the shutters and glanced over at my phone, saw I had several missed calls from the credit card company, and a calendar ping reminding me about dinner with Brian's mother on the other side of town. I couldn't stand her and she was not too fond of me, but I could never say any such thing to him. It was strange that he wasn't home yet—maybe he'd gone straight there? I looked her up in my contacts and called her, fearing I'd have to remind her who I was.

"Oh thank goodness," she answered, "you found his phone."

"Excuse me?" I asked. "Mrs. Hammond, hi, it's me. I'm sorry, I'm running a bit late. Is Brian already there?"

She paused, long enough for me to wonder if maybe she hadn't heard me, then half-covered the microphone but I could hear every word. "It's not someone who found your phone, he's asking if Brian is here, and he's claiming to be you."

"I'll talk to him," Brian said from somewhere in the back of the room.

"No, I'll talk to him," I heard my other self say, and then suddenly he was in my ear. "Hello? Who is this? How do you have my phone?"

Right then I heard the front door shut. "Hello?" Brian called up the stairs.

"I'm just on the line with your mom," I yelled back. The call abruptly cut off. Somewhere in the distance, one set of sirens and then another rose up out the city's usual rush and roar.

"Traffic was crazy, I don't know how I made it home in one piece." I heard him pull off his coat and drop it on the front hall chair. "Is she asking about dinner? Don't tell me she's cancelling."

I stepped out of the bathroom and started down towards him. "I don't know," I said, "I just lost her. Do you have your phone with you?"

"Yes, sure," he said, pulling it out of his pocket. Did this mean he was my Brian? I didn't know what to think. I couldn't tell who was where anymore.

A thud and a crack and another set of sirens, closer this time. A crash?

"Could you maybe give her a call from yours. Mine's been acting up all day. Technology."

I watched as he dialed her number. It rang and rang and rang. "Do you think we should go over there?" he asked.

"I'm sure she'll call back," I said. "Why don't we wait and see if she calls." I went around from room to room, turning off the lights.

"What are you doing?" he asked. "Why are we in the dark?"

"I'm getting a bit of a migraine." I held out my hand. "Let's just sit here on the couch, away from the windows. Let's wait and see if she calls."

He nodded and took my hand, sat down beside me. I let my head fall onto his shoulder.

"Traffic was crazy?" I asked.

"It was," he said. "Worse than I've ever seen it."

A bright flash of light and a loud sharp bang. It could have been from Mrs. Erickson's house. Brian stood up to go to the window and I pulled him back down. "No no, don't do that. Stay here with me. Tell me about your day."

"My day," he said. "My day was good I guess. You know. Apart from the traffic."

I pulled him close, and we heard the key turn in the front door lock, and our hands tightened together as the inside door swung open.

Invasive Species

Mary Kuryla

A BLOATED THING squished under Polly's foot and she lifted her leg at the knee but saw nothing, only water from the showerhead filling the tub. She set her foot back down and the thing was still there, slimy and placental, and must have glued to the underside of her foot. She folded her foot over to the sole, where three of them lay like black commas across the lines of her arch. Water threaded off her nose and she wobbled and almost fell but she did not let go of her foot. She wedged a chewed fingernail under one black tail, gouging to peel the thing off, then she dropped one tadpole after the other into the drain clotted with her hair and blood. The porcelain bathtub had a trip lever and the clogged strainer stopped the water from draining out. Polly did not mind about the clog, about the water held there, but she was beginning to feel shame about the things that slipped in.

Were more of them on her socks? Her socks were in the freezer.

Polly stood barefoot on the deck before the open freezer and set the chilled sock back on top of the waders folded stiff inside. She lowered the lid of the chest. Nothing living or dead on their clothing or gear and how could there be? Before her teammate went off to her own cabin, they had hosed down socks and boots and measuring pole, all the equipment, then dropped each piece in a bucket of salt water, rinsed it through a decon solution and stacked the gear in the freezer. They had done this to rid the gear of lakebed dirt, hidden clingers and vermin too small for the eye to see—contaminants, as her teammate would say.

Maybe they had hosed them off the socks and onto the deck and not noticed, but the tadpoles had seen and they had glued onto her foot. Polly's eyes cut side to side across the cement deck of the Ranger cabin. She could have been looking for those commas that wriggled onto the white page when she had worked at the newspaper, sneaky things that made you think you had made a good sentence when you hadn't. None on the deck and not a tadpole curled in the hose and she lifted her foot again to look if maybe another one had got stuck on. The sun dropped behind the horizon in a shiver, this was late summer in the Sierra.

Polly's job and her teammate's too was to dig out a vernal pool in the bank of a dried lakebed for the yellow-legged frog the State Park grew in a lab because this frog had made it, gotten its name on a govt list. Building a fishless puddle for the yellow-legged tadpoles meant hauling water from a wet lake to a dried one, making sure that no local tadpoles got in. Even one local tadpole in the pool would not be good. Despite the snowpack in the Sierra, they had easily found a dried lakebed in under a half mile of hiking up the range north of their cabins. Polly had found it, really, while her teammate caught her breath at a lower plateau. Her teammate was pregnant with her second, but the air up here was too thin for a thing growing inside you and sucking up your oxygen.

Did the tadpoles on her foot begin as eggs folded in the thick sticky jelly that pulped out of a bullfrog? That would be bad, very bad. Polly walked back inside the cabin for another look in the tub. A black ink body the size of a teardrop was hard to make out in water this clogged. The bottom of the tub was silted in lakebed dirt and strands of her black hair. The water her teammate had given birth in to her first child probably looked a lot like this when all was said and done and the baby flowed out the mother's sewer tunnel into the waters of the birthing tub where it could frolic—that was the word her teammate had used, *frolic*, like a colt does and she was a cowgirl—until the baby catcher hooked fingers around the head and yanked the newborn up into the air. The water her teammate

had birthed in had probably been as bloody as this water backed
up and settled in her bathtub. But did her teammate's birth water
smell like the red russet of a creature unfurled? Did it smell that
good?

~

BETWEEN BITES OF SOFT-BOILED EGG, Polly brushed her teeth over
the tub, toothpaste drooling past her jaw into the water as she
looked for the tadpoles amid tangles of hair and the clumps of
ruby tissue shelled like secret suckers at the bottom. A night had
passed, they should have gassed and bellied up by now. Then
again, maybe the tadpoles had burst in the wee hours and sunk
already all undone to the bottom of the tub. More likely they were
just playing at hiding. Sometimes a puddle could play with you
when the bottom got carpeted with the bodies of black tadpoles so
new and still, tails woven with each other to make one breathing
being under the puddle skin so you got fooled into seeing the
outlines of a freakish swamp fetus lying and waiting to tug you
under. Amphibians don't have fetuses, her teammate would have
told her, and that was why Polly kept her mouth shut and let her
teammate do the knowing.

All at once something wriggled in the water, writing a coin-size
circle in the oily film on the surface. Polly sat on the toilet lid to get
a closer look. The thing's tail flicked at the surface of water like a
hair come to life. That's what it had done—it had come back to
life. The tadpole on her arch had been dead but a night's soak in a
tub clogged with the salvage of her body had given the thing what
it needed to come back to life. She dropped to her knees and
spread her arms over the lip of the tub to embrace the porcelain.
Maybe not the other tadpoles but this one lived and that meant
there was hope.

"The bullfrog is an invasive never identified as far north as the
Sierra," her teammate said when Polly told her about the black
commas dried on her arch. "Call them tadpoles," her teammate
said.

Her teammate's mustard-colored uniform had popped open
over her belly, and she took care to rebutton the shirt before
informing Polly that all local frogs, the yellow-legged excluded,

must be considered invasive species and destroyed. She told Polly to run a quality test for dissolved oxygen levels in the lakebed's remaining waterholes.

"Why bother? The trout fry and local tadpoles in those holes are gulping. They look pretty low. They know it's maybe a day before they dry out." Even Polly, not much more than an intern, could feel the needling heat of the sun that sooner or later dried up everything.

"This may be a drought-ridden tarn with lethargic specimen, but it does not stop us from doing our job." Her teammate often told Polly of her duties, and why not? Her teammate had a degree in biology among other degrees. Get enough degrees and a person collects all the words for saying what needs doing, and in the right way to say it, like the right way to deliver a baby is in water and, if you do not, if you deliver your baby into the cold air of a hospital room then. Well. Polly did not rightly know what happened, not having finished a baby. She was only good at starting them.

Polly thrust the measuring tool into the shallow waterhole in the lakebed though plainly there was not enough water in it to breathe. The tails of the black commas flicking the surface said it all. More water, they said, or we will drown. Sunlight shone off the tadpoles' heads and formed a dozen black eyes staring at her. She stared back.

At dusk the waterhole with the staring tadpoles was dry. The sun had baked the tadpoles onto the shale in the black puncture marks of the oldest language that told what to do. Take us to your bathwaters, they told her. Not exactly protocol, but it just might work. One of the dead had come to life in her tub, why not these? Polly's fix on the world slipped a little out from under her and the slippery thought worked its way in even deeper. Okay, sure, she was no biologist but she didn't need a degree to do an experiment, c'mon, basic school stuff. She could try. She scooped up the dried local tadpoles with a cup then shook the catch into an empty thermos and capped and shoved the thermos inside her kit. Her teammate did not see what Polly had done.

The fact that Polly was even working in these mountains was a fluke. Someone had dropped out last minute and the Park Rangers were prepared to take anyone they could get. They got Polly, who had liked the idea of two women teamed up in the wild. But she and her teammate had never found their rhythm. Of late Polly's teammate only paid mind to the fit of her uniform, her fingers caressing the gold formed button that strained over her belly. Polly admired how unexpectedly fancy the buttons were for a thing as mild as a park uniform, but her teammate could only complain about the uniform. "A pregnant person requires proper gear to etc.," she said. "In the capacity of a pregnant person, a uniform ought to etc." Polly's teammate stood spraddle-legged in the lowest point of the tarn—*tarn*, the word her teammate used for a mountain lake—as high winds gusted off with her words.

The lakebed was uncannily like Polly's bathtub, and her teammate stood now in the low point of the drain. From there the walls of the lakebed rose stories high, only shortening toward shore, but they were not pocked or crumbly. The lake looked newly drained. The ground hadn't scaled yet, here and there a tree without leaves, a boulder, a tailless squirrel showing skull, the bones of an old-time baby carriage tilting out of the dirt.

Her teammate spread her arms out and turned her face to the sun because nutrients from the sun were good for growing a baby. Her teammate's other child, the one that had flowed out of her into the waters of a birthing tub, was now in the hands of her husband. That was good of him since her teammate had a passion for the mountains and for the frogs that hugged them. Her teammate needed this work to stay sane, she said, but her teammate did not do the work, and really not. Her teammate talked about doing work, mostly she talked about teamwork and when she was not talking about teamwork, she was using the right team word to name their duties that she now delegated to Polly since hiking the Sierra looking for a frog that had made a govt list or digging fishless puddles for the tadpoles of that listed frog was impossible when your uniform no longer fit because you were a pregnant person.

THE DRIED tadpoles slipped without ado into the clogged waters of Polly's bathtub. Evening sun through the slats of the shades cut stripes across the water. The tadpoles sunk between this slat and that. It did not hurt anybody and frogs either to put these little dried up dead bodies in her bathtub. It did not even hurt the govt since these ones were local, on nobody's list. The others were safe in the fishless puddle she had dug out from the dried lakebed while her teammate had looked on. The govt-listed tadpoles would soon get good yellow legs, and Polly warmed at the knowledge that creatures had once also grown inside her, gilled at first and then they too had got legs.

All week Polly had been peeling tadpoles off rocks and storing them in her thermos to bring home and slip into her tub, but not another tadpole had wriggled to the surface of the oily waters. Only one had come back to life, the first one, and it still frolicked somewhere in the water. But what this really was? It was a big nothing, a quirk, the tadpole had never been dead, must have been dormant—*dormant*, a word her teammate had used when warning Polly of the latent waters that traveled subterranean limestone routes beneath the mountain tarns. All the dried-up tadpoles she had peeled off tarn rocks and dropped into her tub were dead, real and true.

Polly stripped off her uniform and lifted one foot and then the other into the bathwater and allowed the blood winding down her inner thighs to join with the blood stopped up in the tub, telling herself, Don't be sad, a school experiment, since when did she think she could make life? The blood winding down her legs was the road her fetus traveled to get out of her body. There was still more road to come. This was not her first time of roads, so she knew how the blood came. Polly bent her knees and sank to her chin in the redblack muddy water that smelled of soil, the kind you laid in. The smell pit her teeth.

"A water pump and a battery, the 50 lb. battery, should suffice for the yellow-legged's habitat," her teammate said before they had parted at twilight. One hand on her stomach, the other on her back, her teammate talked about how she never should have slogged the water pump up to the lakebed. Her teammate had left Polly to drag the battery out of the truck's payload and then down a steep wall into the lakebed. Doing it solo had made Polly's blood come on again. The blood had wet through the crotch of her blue uniform.

"Do you talk to it?" Polly asked once she had dragged the battery within shouting distance of her teammate.

"The pump will aerate the water in the habitat," her teammate said. "Aerated water evaporates at a high rate. We'll have to haul in more water from the wet lake."

"Talk to him in there." Polly set down the battery and strode up to her teammate to poke the formed gold button where the uniform gaped.

Her teammate took a step back from Polly. "Like talk to tadpoles? Go ahead, talk to them. The point is oxygen."

"Talk to the baby growing in you is what I'm talking about," Polly said.

"Yes, I talk to my baby. She likes my talk a lot. Bach, too."

"I talk to the dead. To all the ones that didn't come." Polly touched her crotch and her teammate's eyes lowered to the stain.

"Like miscarried?"

"I've been shedding placenta and baby all week," Polly said. "Will you come talk to the dead, like you talk to your baby?"

Her teammate stopped looking at Polly. She said she was deeply sorry for Polly's loss, it's best to focus on work. Tomorrow they would stake the battery and chain it. "The setup is basically an aquarium. Do that and they will live."

In the bathwater Polly sat with the dead. She dropped her head back onto the lip of the tub to listen to the Bach she had put on the player before getting in with the bodies of tadpoles she peeled off the walls of waterholes. What had her teammate said about Bach? Point, counterpoint? Polly promised herself that one day she would sit in a tub chock full of living tadpoles, not these little empty comma sacks, stop with the dead stuff, everything in the tub dead. Polly dozed off in a thrilling delicacy of cellos but then a thing slinked past her foot and woke her. Must have been that one living tadpole. But another one wiggled and whipped her thigh. Nothing moved in the blood water, but even so all around her there came a feeding a harmony a sponge on the blood. More wriggling between her toes. They squirmed into her butt crack and nipped at the deep folds in between her thighs. They nested in her belly. This was life, life breathed into the tadpoles, she was sure of it. On her blood and her tissue and her hair and a bit of lake dirt in bath water, the tadpoles had come back to life and the Bach had done it.

Polly had once seen in a shallow creek a drowned lizard haired with black commas. The million mouths, not egg and not yet frog, suckling on lizard scales soaked to the color of milk. The tails of the tadpoles flicking in bright feast. The memory of the lizard eaten up like that made the thrill at bringing the tadpoles back to life slip into fright. Polly clasped the sides of the tub. She wanted out of the bog. A suck and a heel slip on the slimed tub floor and all she managed was to get the tips of her shoulders out. The things inside did not want her to go, and it would require a lot of force to lurch her whole torso out of the black mass. The pulling out of herself, the doing of it, landed her on her head on the linoleum.

COLD WATER SPLASHED Polly's throat. Her eyes opened on a view of the underlip of the tub. Why was she on the floor? She lifted her head but her neck no longer wanted much to do with her head. Teamwork had stopped between head and neck. Her skull hit the linoleum and it didn't hurt too bad because she was lying in water. That smell again, circulating the shallow puddle where she lay, pit her teeth. Another splash from out of the tub sprayed gouts of black water across her cheeks. Now a long tail thick as her arm and tapering at the tip eeled over the lip of the tub to hook the porcelain fold.

She rolled away from the tub and banged her forehead into the toilet. She used the base to pull onto her knees then swivel her ass onto the seat to get a better look at whatever that was in the tub. The bend of her head on her neck fed the view of the thing aslant. It was blubbered as a marine mammal, color of indigo, black grape, reddest at the tail that hooked to the tub. Swolled lips sucked the last of the tub's fluids. What it hadn't gulped up had spilled out and onto the linoleum as it got big as a garbage sack, and the thing looked like it was not done doing whatever it was doing in the way of getting big. She could not know how big. Bile eked out her crooked mouth. Polly hoped soon to stop gagging.

She wore waders and boots stiff and still iced from the freezer to drag the thing by the tail out of the tub and across the floor through the cabin's front door. The tail was muscled and vibrated between her oiled hands and she held to it like to a colt at the other end of a tether. Red lumps of tissue smeared the wood slats she dragged it over. Sure, maybe it was hurt, look at the gunk leaking out its holes, it groaned and snuffled but it was not dying. It was growing. But right now, it was no friend of the air and that was the advantage she still held over it. She dragged it across the deck toward the truck.

Polly and her teammate had used large foam tubes to brace the 50 lb. battery when the truck drove over the bumpy track to the lake. The thing from the tub sucked in gulps on a foam tube in the payload, which she had managed to get it into with the help of the automatic lift and good thick rope from the truck.

She backed up the truck to the edge of the dried lakebed, no easy job with her head bent off her neck like it was. She walked round to the rear where the pink dawn had glossed the thing russet. The frayed tip of the good thick rope hung out of its mouth. The foam tubes were sucked out and curled on the truck bed in cast-off skin sacks. The thing had gotten too big to drag out, but she had to get rid of it, and she could not harm it with her own hands, stab it or run it over, the dry droughted lakebed killed everything sooner or later. She opened the tailgate and the thing lunged for her. Though her arms swung open of their own will for a hug, her legs bucked and reared. She would have fallen down the steep wall of the lakebed if her boot hadn't caught at a stone ledge. The thing slopped off the truck and rolled past her moaning and croaking along the lake wall in a commotion of slack stones.

SUNLIGHT SLATTED the wall above Polly's bed, beside which her teammate now stood looking down at her. "You should lock your front door, anything can slip in. That's how I got in. There's a battery to stake and it's really past noon."

Nothing in the lakebed looked anything like the thing she had dumped there at dawn. There was the sapling that thrust from the lake wall, the boulder, and the baby carriage. No sign of the squirrel or its skull. She wondered if the wood floor of her cabin was still smeary with what had come off the thing. Half asleep, still clinging to her dreams, she had hurried after her teammate out the cabin door without noticing the floors. Could all have been another of those dreams that caused her to sleep sort of contorted, and that was why her head bent funny off her neck.

Her teammate did not mention the slant of Polly's neck because her teammate was occupied with pointing at the yellow-legged tadpoles squirming in the shallow waters of the puddle Polly had dug. "They are at risk of desiccation. The status of the juveniles' habitat is dire."

"I'll fetch water from the other lake."

"Stake the battery first."

Polly understood that her teammate had given her a directive. She was to drive the three-inch wide post into the dried lakebed to which they would chain the battery that juiced the pump's air supply to the puddle. Polly said, "This feels like a bad idea."

But when she said it, she was not looking at her teammate to see how her words went over. It was the lake wall that had her attention. Tire marks grooved the bank. The thing had lunged at her there from the rear of the truck. Yeah, she was sure, and that was the stone jutting out of the lake wall below the tracks that had caught her boot and stopped her fall. But where was the creature? Had it gotten bigger or was it pruned-up dead somewhere in the sun? So long as the lake stayed dry and the sun stayed high, the thing would not have a chance of surviving. She wanted to feel happy about it dying but instead she missed the scent of it in her tub. Was this feeling borne of a mother's love or was it awe for a thing that had come to seem strangely ancient, even inevitable? Was the thing souled? Her momentary tenderness morphed into frank horror at the possibility.

Her teammate thrust the stake-pointed end of the post into the lakebed and made a cut. "Staking is the most stable option," she said. "I'll hold it in place for you." Her teammate toed in her direction a mallet she had dragged up here while Polly was sleeping in.

Polly squatted beside the mallet to take up the handle. Her mind should be on teamwork, but it was not, she was thinking about how in the night she had wrapped her hands around the thing's tail and thrilled at the vitality of it—it was sick—not the thing, her, she was one messed-up Polly. Hadn't the tadpoles wanted her to stay in the tub? But she didn't stay, she got out scared, and when the clotted bathwaters congealed to give birth to what she had started, she didn't even have the character to keep it as her own.

The lakebed panted and seethed under her boots. All the way

to her soles, Polly felt the mallet was wrong. Banging a post was wrong wrong wrong. She dropped the mallet and stood. "How long can a tadpole breathe outside of water?" she asked.

"The tadpole's skin has pores that respirate to remove hydrogens from the oxygens," said her teammate, spacing each word as if she spoke to a child. "Don't concern yourself. Drive the post in."

"I can't lift the mallet with my neck like this," Polly said. "Let's skip the whole thing."

Her teammate eyed the puddle of yellow-legged frogs. The tadpoles gave hopeless kisses to the water's surface. Polly could see her teammate was getting spiritually edgy about the drying puddle. "Look, I'm holding the post," her teammate said. "You bang it. That's teamwork. Do it."

"You do it."

Her teammate's lips swelled to a pout. She patted the place on her uniform that puckered around the gold button. "Bump."

Hot spokes of rage flared up Polly's arms. She grasped the handle and hoisted the mallet up and swung it wild over her head so her cowering teammate had to twist on her hips to defend her belly but still she held onto the post. The mallet landed true on the head of the post and bulleted it deep into the lakebed. The shaft of the post vanished. It left a short head.

Her teammate squared her shoulders for a good scold of Polly. Enough was enough, really and etc.

Polly tried to pay attention to the good teamwords flowing out of her teammate's mouth. If only the water that pooled around the staked post didn't look so much like blood seeping from a nail riven in the palm of a hand.

The water broke. It rushed up from below the dried bed, rising so fast it took her teammate another sentence to stop talking and start feeling the water pouring into her boots. They pivoted toward shore but by then the water was at their waists. Animals floated out of their burrows in the caked banks and paddled to get ahead of the water, a mole surfaced and slapped unseeing alongside them. Polly felt unexpectedly good stroking in consonance with her teammate. Chances of making it to the truck parked at the shallow end were good.

Something waved the water under Polly's thighs, and it was not the water rising from whatever subterranean limestone routes flowed in dumb momentum below, no. This thing under her thighs, what she felt going by, took time to pass, the way a longish and largish fish would take. She swam faster. Was her teammate keeping up? She looked back but did not see her, or see only her teammate—it was there, too. A hole on the water, black gap, stirred by a red meaty ribbon rotating out. Polly's arm stopped on a stroke. All of her got lost and could not bother. It was the post, the driving of it into the dried bed, it was the water rushing up that had brought the thing to life, and this living thing was hers and hers alone.

Water folded over Polly's head, she went under, and she was glad because she had gotten it wrong. The tadpoles eating the lizard drowned in the creek had made the lizard look haired but it wasn't hair. The tadpoles had fattened themselves on lizard parts until they could sprout their own limbs. A thing had to be sacrificed for another to live.

An arm ringed her neck and yanked her to the surface. Her teammate's hand propped Polly's head above water, and Polly coughed up a glob of filth into her teammate's hair, grateful as hell to be saved from drowning. *A tarn, a tarn, are they worth a darn?* The silly rhyme came to Polly, and she heard her own voice fold round her teammate's in the song of the tarn. Black cloud by black cloud, Polly blinked at the sky, cradled in the woman's arm. Her boot slipped off her idle foot, and she let her dear teammate swim them toward shore. Weren't they both mothers, after all? And her teammate loved the tadpoles and had sacrificed for them in her way, and she did this knowing that all creatures are foreigners to ourselves, their ways of knowing spilling always beyond us, even the human animal growing in a belly.

If only the water would stop its pushing from below. Now her teammate's arm was sliding off Polly's neck. Why let her go—it had been so good, hadn't they finally found their rhythm? Lake water splashed into Polly's mouth. She startled and kicked upright to gain a purchase on her teammate's comforting arm, but her teammate's body had gone off to do something odd. It was cutting across the lake surface like a figure on a ship's prow. Her teammate's face showed shock and her mouth jerked open to tell Polly so, but her teamwords went the way of her spiraled torso. She sunk under. Polly swallowed air and rolled forward into the teaming water and dove into twists of silt. She stroked and kicked into withered roots and got tangled in hair-like vines. Just ahead a mustard-colored uniform sped by as if propelled by jellyfish but as Polly reached through the reddening murk for her teammate, a black tail snuck out of the wake and lassoed the uniform, once and gone.

Polly rose to the surface on a bleed of bubbles. Her lost boot knocked slow across her nose. Polly swallowed another round of air and dove again for her teammate but the rising water was not having it. It unfurled a wave that punched right into Polly, launching her head over feet through the water—but her neck slammed into the sapling thrust out from the lake wall—she reached and grabbed for the sapling—her whole body one with the labor of a lake filling itself back up.

∼

NIGHT, naked in the dark of the porch, Polly hosed off her blue uniform spread arms and legs out on the cabin deck after a dunking in the solution. Good teamwords flowed, decontamination and protocol. Next job, unclog the bathtub, the sooner it drained, the sooner a hot shower. She drew her uniform out of the salt rinse and hosed it off again.

Something was under her foot. She could have pitched through the deck, but instead she paused, thumbed the hose off, thought: could it be the tadpole of the yellow-legged frog? The tadpoles had churned up with her and her teammate when the water broke. Maybe one had stuck to her arch and all the teamwork they did for the govt list would not be lost. For her teammate's sake, Polly hoped this was so. She lifted her foot but nothing was there on the deck. She folded her foot over, and all at once the porch light sparked on, but Polly held steady. The formed gold button from her teammate's uniform now stuck to her arch.

Until evening, Polly had lain unconscious on shore with the tip of the sapling clasped in her hand. She only came awake when a thing struck her head. Startled, and swinging up, she landed back on her ass on the bank of the lake, no sign of what had struck her. The lake sat alongside silent as the night's tongue, swollen to indigo. The creature frolicked now under the lake waters despite her small mothering cowardice and lust for her own species.

Though she would never know the thing true, she had given it life. But the doing of it had surely been a severing from her own kind.

A last thin fold of light behind the truck parked at the shore no more than a hundred feet away. Polly had got there on hands and knees. Her teammate was on the ground, curled all the way around the truck's back wheel, and she might have spotted her sooner had she worn the mustard-colored uniform but the uniform must have flowed off her teammate once the creature got its mouth on for a good suck. Her teammate was pocked and husked, not a femur not a bone, a skin sack.

Polly lifted the lid of the freezer chest and looked in, in the palm of her hand, the button. Her teammate was folded stiff beside the waders inside. She would want her button with her. Polly murmured a few good words and placed her teammate's gold on the bump in the fold.

A Cruelty

Rory Say

I WAS HALF FROZEN by the time my father called for a stop. We stood outside a building. More intact than most in the area, it was a wide, two-storey structure, its front face made of the same dull brick as the walls to either side. An orange light buzzed in the entryway, and a few of the windows that weren't boarded by planks glowed as well. Mutely, I watched my father fold up and pocket his directions, then take from the same pocket a key the size of a long twig. I followed him down the footpath.

The front door, opaque with clouded glass, yielded noisily at the turning of the key. Damp, dusty air met us as we entered. A shaded lamp stood in a corner, partly illuminating a predominantly shadowed foyer—armchairs to either side, a full-length mirror reflecting the slate greyness of the opposite wall, a staircase to our right, ahead and to our left a hallway whose passage dissolved into shadow.

My father muttered something about the stairs and then moved toward them. Beneath us a rough carpet absorbed our footfalls, and it seemed as we ascended that the only sound in the whole building was the pulse of blood between my ears.

The upper floor was no better lit than the first. Doors lined a dim hall that ran to our left and right. Without pausing to consider, my father led me by the wrist to the second door on our left, gave three brisk raps, then immediately opened it and pulled me inside.

What was my first impression of these rooms which were to house us? Darkness, I suppose, a shade deeper than out in the hall. Still, I could tell by the crowded shapes on the white walls, and by some general aura of abundance, that the place was densely packed and cluttered.

My father instructed that I stay where I was until he came right back. I watched his shadowed shape disappear through what I took to be a small kitchen to our right, and a few seconds later he returned to report that his uncle was asleep and must not be disturbed. I nodded invisibly. Around a corner we found another unlit room, a single bed against the far wall. My father closed the door behind us.

Exhaustion struck me with the force of a blow. Dropping my bag, I crossed the room and flung myself on the stiff mattress, where I lay on my stomach and devoured the sandwiches which earlier I'd been too ill to eat on the bus. Meanwhile, my father struggled to find a working light. I paid no attention. Life drained pleasantly from my limbs as I ate in the dark, the day behind me condensed and oddly remote. Only the ache in my legs was proof of the distance we'd covered, the black taste of vomit from the rattling bus ride which lingered in my mouth even after the sandwiches were gone.

I rolled on my side. A window above my head showed a dusting of early stars, a rising moon that itself looked ill. My father had given up trying to find a light and was presently relieving himself next door. We traded places when he returned, and afterwards I found him half-covered on the bed, turned to the wall beneath the window. I paused before approaching. By the moon's anaemic light he looked horridly exposed, his thin shoulders almost as white as the sheet that came to his waist. Between them I could see the jutting ridge of his spine.

He did not stir when I crawled in beside him, nor when I squirmed out of my clothes and pushed them to the floor. Had sleep taken him so suddenly? I imagined instead that his heart had stopped, or perhaps been gripped by some spectral hand in my absence and wrung of its blood. Did I lay now next to the corpse of my father? Or what if—surely worse—my father was no longer in the room? What if I leaned over the body at my back only to find the face of a stranger?

I held myself very still. A cold patch of moonlight lay beneath me on the carpet, and I watched as the passing of minutes caused it to drift imperceptibly toward the door.

~

SOME WHILE LATER I found myself walking in the dark. But where? I had no memory of rising from bed and leaving the room, and yet here I was, alone in a different room, one that was larger than the one I had left, one with a wider window out of which I could see the same slab of skull-coloured moon whose faint imprint I'd been monitoring on the carpet only a moment ago. Or what felt like a moment ago.

I came to a stop. Had I slept? My mind tingled with the feeling that I could leap from the highest building and land like a feather on the ground, and yet I was not dreaming. I was awake and aware in a strange room with a man seated in front of me.

Not even when I noticed him did my fear return. He sat in a corner to the left of the window, motionless, ensconced in near-total dark. It was no wonder I had missed him; all I could make out was the side of his head nearest the moon. My gaze fixed now on what looked like a great hole where his eye should be, but which I saw after a moment was only the round lens on a pair of dark spectacles.

Was he blind? I felt a sudden thrill at the thought of observing this man, who I'd begun to reason must be my father's uncle, without myself being seen. Inching closer on silent feet, I came near enough to touch him and stopped. Something repelled me. No part of the man had yet perceptibly moved, and it was easy to imagine that he would remain this way until dawn, until the following night and the following dawn. I thought of my father as I had last seen him. I thought of myself in a dead house housing only the dead, and I felt a second thrill at the thought that I—

Fingers touched my face. I had not seen the hand rise between us; nor did I turn or cry out at the feel of the touch, a touch which stilled the very workings of my insides. I can still feel it now, the fingertips bony and pointed on my cheek. Instinctively I reached for the hand at the wrist and felt it go limp as it dropped to the shadowed lap. All thereafter was still. The man's head, drooped somewhat, had not moved, and after a few seconds I found myself retreating the way I had apparently come. Behind me the seated man remained as I had found him.

The door to my room stood ajar. In the bed my father, or a body that had taken his place, still lay facing the wall, pale shoulders almost luminous beneath the window. Sliding under the sheets, I felt at once dazed and alert, suspended in a dream from which I knew only sleep could wake me. There was no moon left on the carpet.

∾

COLD SUNLIGHT FILLED the window when next I looked. I stretched myself, momentarily oblivious, a tingling in the knees of my sore legs. My arm struck the wall beside me. I was alone in bed.

Everything then came back in a flood. I sat up and found my father, alive and intact, balancing on one bare foot as he pulled a sock over the other. Noticing me, he began to talk about having to leave, but as I tried to listen I became aware of something wrong with my face. My mouth felt funny. A coppery tang made my thoughts recoil.

Beside me my father, now buckling yesterday's pants, asked what was wrong. I put two fingers in my mouth and removed a tooth, a loose molar from the lower left side. There was no pain despite the blood.

It meant good luck, my father said. He continued dressing himself, hurried but clumsy. By the red whites of his eyes he looked unslept. His fingers raked his thin hair as he picked up the jacket he'd dropped on the floor the previous evening. He had to go out for a while, he said, and see about some work.

No argument came to me. Work was what my father had been seeing about for some time. I suspected that a lack of it was why we were here, the reason we'd fled our old building and come to this one, though I knew well that the subject was delicate. I only asked if there was any food, and my father, preoccupied and impatient, searched one bag, then another, and produced at length a couple of crushed sandwiches which he tossed on my lap. He'd be back later, he said. I was not to touch anything. And there was no need to worry, he added, pausing at the door, because I would not be alone.

With these words he left me. I could make out his voice briefly in the living room, and then the sound of the front door opening and gently closing. Quiet fell. I still sat in bed, my tooth held out as if for someone to see. How odd to think of it gone, out of my head and here in my hand. Carefully, I put the point of its root in the hole in my gums and locked my jaw. It felt like nothing back inside me; if I never opened my mouth again, it would be as if I'd never lost it.

Sliding from bed, I dressed quickly from the pile of clothes beside me. It was too cold in the room, which in the soft daylight looked to be part of some private museum, or ossuary—scattered on every surface were bones of various type and size. I gathered that all were related to forms of sea life, given that here and there stood the complete skeleton of a fish impaled on a wire stand. Huge-mouthed skulls hung also from the walls, as did bits of netting, strands of rope, knives thin and hefty, the hooked end of a harpoon mounted by the door.

These things I studied with a kind of blank wonder. Never in my life had I seen the sea; these bones I prodded or picked up might as well have come from outer space. Without allowing myself to hesitate, I let my curiosity lead me to the living room, where I found the same man I had met in the night.

He sat just as he had then, statue-still in a chair by the window. It occurred to me in that moment that my father and I had commandeered the only bedroom.

How shall I tell you of his appearance? He was old, certainly, though to what extent I found it hard to guess. For one thing he was hairless. I had glimpsed the smooth side of his face in the moonlight, but now I could see that the whole of his head was bald as an egg. As before, it was tilted slightly forward, so that his covered eyes seemed fixed on some point between us. (There was no sign that my presence in the room was noticed.) He wore a muddied leather vest over a plain white shirt buttoned to the neck, with brown trousers whose bottom hems came to the heels of his wool-stockinged feet. His skin, where visible, was reddened and looked rough. In place of a mouth was a sealed, downcurved seam, above which loomed a nose like a red pitted gourd. In stature he was no larger than my father, though his body, perhaps on account of its striking inertia, conveyed to me a sense of weight beyond its size, of great density, as though his veins coursed not with blood but liquid stone. I imagined that he was not only unmoving but unmovable.

Then something awful happened. Slowly, so that it took a second to be sure that what I saw was real, the old man's mouth peeled itself open in either an enormous yawn or howl of silent agony, and as I stared from where I stood I glimpsed a single tooth lodged at the back of his lower jaw. My tongue probed the hole in my own mouth—the tooth I'd put back was gone.

Just then the front door opened. I looked for my father but found instead two women coming into the room. Both wore long green coats and had the same tight bun of hair at the back of their heads, one light, one dark. They glared at me. One of them asked who I was and, utterly bewildered, I heard myself mumble a few words about my father and my father's uncle, about the bus we'd taken here from somewhere far away. This seemed only to confuse them. Each gave me a wary look as they came further into the room, placed bags on the floor, and soon began feeding the man in the chair spoonfuls of a colourless paste they'd brought with them.

A fluttering sickness passed through my stomach. Silently I went to the bedroom, where I sat at the edge of the bed and brought to mind my missing tooth in the old man's mouth. There was no doubt it was the very same one. I had the sense as in a nightmare of being involved in something both improbable and inevitable. Where I sat was unsafe. I could hear the strange women in the other room conversing in low tones as though plotting murder, and I wondered whether it was myself they discussed.

Snatching the sandwiches my father had left, I crept from the room and slipped out the front door. If anyone heard me, nobody followed. It was quiet in the hall. I rushed down the carpeted stairs and flew outdoors as if escaping a fire.

I ran in the opposite direction from which we'd come the night before, remembering the labyrinth of alleys we'd navigated only with my father's handwritten directions. There was nobody about.

My lungs burned inside me, though the air was bitingly cold, colder even than it had been yesterday. I had forgotten my jacket. Realising this, I slowed, and for a moment considered turning back. But I had no key. And why should I want to turn back? At least the possibility of help lay ahead, or so I told myself. I kept going at a halfhearted pace.

How far did I go? And what difference in the end did the distance make? The street, it seemed, went on and on, a straight or curving line that gradually rose or lightly dipped; rarely could I see far ahead or behind. Nor did any of the buildings I passed lend the impression of occupancy.

When my legs and lungs gave out I slowed, and almost immediately my teeth began clattering in my skull. Overhead the day's leaden roof was scarred with bars of silver light, and all my skin felt as an open wound in the raw, cutting breeze. I slowed further, then stopped.

Against a low stone wall I sank down and hugged my knees. I ate half of one sandwich but couldn't finish. My throat felt seared with cold, and by now I was shaking almost violently. More than anything I'd become overwhelmingly tired, fatigued in the very roots of my bones. My eyes blinked themselves shut, and perhaps I dozed.

It was almost dark by the time my father came down the street.

FOR DAYS or weeks I lay drowned in burning sleep, surfacing only for bouts of fevered consciousness. That I had not died was in no way clear to me. Then I understood: I'd been rescued from one nightmare and restored to another, the bed in the room in the building.

I recall my father in the room, tepid water held to my lips, food I would swallow and reject. Sometimes he was there and sometimes he was gone, out, I suppose, in his usual search for work. Once or twice a tall man was with him, long mournful face, cold instruments pressed to my bare chest and head, a prodding at the back of my throat. I had heard of doctors but he was the first I had seen. Pneumonia, I later learned, as well as undernourishment— weak of chest and brittle of bone. No response came to me when he said, in a deep serious voice, that I should count myself very lucky.

It seemed at the time a cruel thing to say. Was it luck that had lost me more parts of myself? Two toes and the tip of each pinky. Also half my voice. I spoke thereafter how I imagined a ghost might speak, in a quietly harsh scratching whisper, painful to get out. In this voice I told my father the truth of his uncle, the reason I'd fled headlong and jacketless into the freezing unknown. In this voice I begged to be taken away.

My father's reaction surprised me. I needed rest, he insisted, interrupting. Quiet now, hush. Rest, sleep, recover. Then, when my persistence dashed any hope that my words were no more than the ravings of one whose soul has tread so near to death, he grew quiet and frightened. I saw it in his eyes, in his face which sank. The ordeal, he feared, had robbed me of mind as well as body.

His uncle, he tried patiently to explain, was exactly as he seemed. He was a man who'd lived a long, difficult life at sea and nowadays required help on account of some illness having cost him his sight. Most of his time was spent at rest, and speaking of which—

At *sea*? I sat up with a questioning look. Yes, my father said. Hadn't I seen the artifacts around this place? His uncle had been a whaler, which meant a whale hunter. In the past men killed whales for things inside them—meat, ivory, bone, blubber. Whatever else. A whale's body is a very big vessel, and certain things inside are worth a price.

Cautiously, I considered this, things inside worth a price. It was clear that my father's aim was to endear his uncle in my eyes, and yet the longer I turned over this bedside tale in my head, the colder I became. Here was a man who'd made his living harvesting the sea for its bodies, the bodies for their parts. My eyes flitted to the proof about the room—the bone menagerie adorning the dresser past my feet; the mounted gaping mouths; dead gaze of empty sockets. With still-numb fingertips I touched my left cheek and felt a faint sting. A foul taste filled my mouth.

Oblivious, my father rose from my side and wordlessly left the room. I gave a cry that rose no higher than a whimper, and suddenly I was alone. What would happen to me? Would my body continue to be quietly plundered, losing its components until I too was no more than a cage of bones on a mantle? A skull gazing from—

My father reappeared in the doorway. He had something to show me, he said, something that would help. I shook my head and he smiled with desperate encouragement. Then he stepped aside. Someone was next to him, a shorter man who now replaced him in the doorway. I was so shocked to see him upright that it took a moment to identify my father's uncle. He stood unsteadily, knees trembling. The sight wiped clean my thoughts. I stared from where I lay, watching as the old man raised a hand and very slowly removed his dark glasses, revealing eyes partially whited between wilted lids. His mouth twitched into a kind of smile.

Then he spoke.

It was not the words themselves that struck me, but the voice— a quietly harsh scratching whisper. In the other half of my own voice, my father's uncle at last welcomed me into his home. I screamed until I fainted.

~

THE MAN with the mournful face returned to my side. This time he pricked my arm for its blood and looked once more in my mouth, which bled when open and tasted at all times vile. Contaminated socket, he uttered, pinching my chin to turn my head. He soaked a cotton wad in clear fluid and pressed it burning to my gums. Behind him my father fidgeted.

The doctor had questions which I did my best to answer. I told him about my tooth and where he could find it, about the stolen half of my voice which even now lay trapped in a man's mouth in the next room. His hand left my face. It was nothing, my father said, stepping nearer. My mind was sick with fever and lately I had not been myself.

It struck me that the heart of this was true; lately I had not been my entire self. How much must one lose, I wondered, before what's lost outweighs what remains? At what stage does the self give way? With my eyes I conveyed as best I could my plight to the doctor, who still regarded me with measured concern. Would he help? After a moment he sat back, then rose to lead my father by the arm out to the hall. For some minutes I listened to their conspiring voices beyond the closed door, but I could make out no words. What had I done, I asked myself, to warrant such cruelty?

Again I cried out in my broken voice and again was unheard. Then with a sudden lurch I flung myself to the clothes-strewn floor. My legs felt boneless, my right foot still bandaged after the amputation of two dead toes. For a moment I lay in a heap, steeling myself, before I began crawling painfully toward the door. The two voices moved away as if repelled by my approach, and a second later I heard them joined by a third in the living room, a faint scraping on my ears. My blood froze, and my body with it. Then, planting one knee on the ground and lifting myself up, I reached for the doorknob but grabbed instead the head of a harpoon from where it hung by two nails on the nearby wall.

The voices dropped to murmurs and fell silent.

I put the thin iron shank in my mouth and bit down, clutching it between my teeth. The cotton wad was still there; faintly I tasted blood and the acrid burn of pain reliever. My head swam. On my backside I dragged myself to the bed, then hoisted myself up, the sheets stiff and yellowed with old sweat. I closed my eyes to the wall when the door opened. It was the doctor. I knew him from my father by his quietly charged authoritative air, by the pressure of his tragic gaze on the back of my head. My own eyes I kept closed, feigning sleep, testing the harpoon's point with the pad of a thumb.

A minute later and the doctor was gone, this time failing to suggest that I count myself lucky.

∾

JUST BEFORE DARK that same day, my father came in and attempted to feed me. He hardly looked well himself. His hands quivered and he kept spilling what I refused to eat on my chest and the bedcovers, until eventually he gave up. I allowed only that he replace my mouth's cotton wad with a fresh one.

Lingering afterwards, I could see his thoughts searching for words which failed him. At last he mentioned his uncle and I turned with a sick groan to the window. My father sighed. His hand found my shoulder and rested there. Things would change, he told me. Already our luck was turning around. Tomorrow he was to begin work at some far-off factory, and the following day we'd go together to a hospital, where I could stay until fully recovered.

I kept my mouth shut, my prize held near to my heart. My father's hand slid away as he bent to reconfigure the nest of clothes and pillows on which he slept, the bed having become my own domain. A part of me pitied him.

He kept talking as he undressed and settled down on the floor, painting for me a picture of what our lives would look like in a few short weeks, months, years. Already our luck was turning around. These words sank into me as I pretended to sleep until I slept.

~

THE ROOM WAS empty when I awoke the next morning. It felt early but might not have been. Above my head the window showed white, and up on my knees I could see the cracked and barren street silvered with frost. My forehead froze on the glass and I remembered what I had held to my chest like a talisman through the night. I searched the sheets and found it at last secreted beneath the pillow, a gift from some guardian fairy. Fingering once more the points on its tip, I wondered what rough beast from what unknowable depths this tool had bled and helped bring to light. Which parts were salvaged and which discarded? I cast my eyes about the shelved and mounted bones surrounding me, and tried to guess which among them had composed just such a creature.

Beneath me the building's front door opened and banged shut, and a moment later the two strange women entered the apartment. This meant I had slept longer than I'd thought. I heard footsteps and hushed voices, and then to my surprise a light knock came to my own door. I sank down and said nothing, but still the door opened and one of the women came in. She had medicine for me, she said, smiling, and also food if I would eat it. Of course I refused both, keeping my mouth clamped shut when she approached with her poison, the harpoon readied in the event that she tried to insist. Luckily she didn't. On her way out she left a few pills and some water on the side table. I waited a while after they'd both gone before trying to stand.

Placing my intact foot down on the floor, I allowed it to take my weight by slow degrees. My head felt faint. I realised I had no clear picture of what lay ahead. Sharp pain shot through my maimed foot when I favoured it, but I found that limping on my heel was tolerable. In this way I went down to the living room.

My father's uncle stood next to his chair with his back to the window, a glass of water shivering in his hand. His face moved toward me, his shaded eyes on the ground between us. Behind him the sun had breached the marble roof of cloud, bathing the room in a harsh radiance. All at once my head cleared and the world came sharply into focus.

The old man spoke my name as though it were a question. His voice was ragged and he coughed to clear it. I gave no response. Water splashed on the carpet as he put his glass on the windowsill and felt for the arm of his chair, and suddenly we were both positioned in just the same way we had been in the depths of that first night. How many nights had it been? Already I found my life before this place distant to memory.

My father's uncle asked if I was feeling better. Was there something I wanted? As in a dream I moved toward him, all my pain forgotten. Sensing me, he reached out a hand which I sidestepped to avoid. He asked again if there was something I wanted and I answered yes. It was the only word I ever spoke to him. I watched as his face looked up, his dark mouth parting. Inside I could see it.

Lifting to his eyes what I had taken from the wall, I turned it in my hand for his sightless appraisal. He began to speak but I stopped him, taking hold of his cheek and pushing gently through the soft skin beneath the opposing ear. Everything went rigid. A kind of groaning sigh filled my head that only afterwards I realised came from the quivering mouth before me. Then the sound stopped and it was over. There was nothing more to push.

I stepped back and looked at what I'd done. It had all happened too quickly, and without, it seemed, my full consent. I felt giddy. My first thought was to leave at once, but when I hobbled to the window I saw that snow now tumbled from a curdled sky, sunless once again. My bones shivered at the sight.

Turning back to the man in the chair, I rested my eyes on his stillness for a moment before setting to work on the difficult task of extracting my tooth, using what blades and plying instruments I could find on the walls about me. It took what felt like an hour. Twice I paused to be sick, and when finally I finished I found to my dismay that the tooth had changed; it was dull and discoloured, its stubby root dark yellow and decayed. When I touched it in my own infected socket, it wouldn't fit and made me bleed pus. What more could I do? I went again to the window and gazed out at the snow, sparse flakes twirling down to extinguish on the pavement.

It was almost dark by the time my father came down the street.

Another Mother Again

Cyan Katz

Finland, 1893

WE LIVE with our father in the forest. I sleep in the hay loft with my twin.

Father sleeps downstairs, alone.

What day is tomorrow, my boys?

July the tenth.

What do we observe on that day?

Our mother's death, we say together.

FATHER WORKS on the railroad tracks, building the rail from Kouvola to Kotka. Every morning at 4 a.m., we wake before Father, stoke the fire, and make breakfast. Always the same breakfast. Eggs and onions, because that's what we always have. We go out to the hen house, gently lift up our hens, Sini, Kukka, Reeta, and Anna, and take their warm, brown eggs back to the house in our baskets.

Sometimes the eggs have two yolks. That's how we know it will be a special day. We open the eggs this morning, July 10th, and discover today is one of those days.

Father leaves and we busy ourselves with the gardening and housework, knowing we must work quickly, so we can have time to spend making The Mother. Summer hours are the most precious for gardening: the ground freezes from October to March.

We've already set out the materials: a broken rocking chair, a pillow full of rotting hay, and some birch branches. The head will come later, it takes more time.

My brother is in charge of baking the bread. The cabin fills with the smell of it, and he's done something new: added caraway seeds. They make me uneasy. The little greenish-black, crescent moon shaped seeds change the smell of the *Ruisleipä*. It becomes even more aromatic, and reminds me of when mother was sick. We ground the dry fruits in our mortar and pestle, making a paste and spreading it on her tongue. It didn't work. Nothing worked. Nothing could stop the illness from taking over her body.

Brother?
(looks)
Do you remember how she looked?
(shakes head)...*Do you?*
No. I can't remember anymore.

A few of the back slats of the rocking chair are broken completely out, and the arms gnawed by carpenter ants. We lash the pillow against the slats, and tie the branches to the pillow with twine. We use the black branches to make her arms.

The bread cools on the table.

I take the candied cherries from the cupboard. Special rubies used once a year and never eaten, only tasted. I open the jar and inhale. I take what will be mother's lips from the jar, a single cherry. I bite it in half, and spit the other half back in the jar for next year. My mouth creates her mouth.

The bread is still cooling.

I can't remember what she looked like but I can remember her hair and her smell. I can remember her hands, with nails too long and knuckles too big. I can remember her hair falling out. I can remember the smell of her sick sweat as she held me. I can remember her nails turning yellow. I hate that she's dead and I hate that I can't remember her face. My stomach turns into a wasp's nest, full of holes and squirming larvae.

I plunge my thumbs into the still-too-hot bread. The steam and hot *Ruisleipä* burn the pads of my thumbs. I don't feel anything on the inside now.

Brother enters quietly from the garden.

He looks at the holes in the bread.

The blisters on my thumbs begin to bubble.

~

THE AIR OUTSIDE turns very cold; not typical for July in our part of the country, when we sleep with cloth over our faces because dark comes so late and leaves so early. The clouds knit across the sky and the wind whispers against the quaking aspen leaves, "soon soon soon."

It begins to rain.

Father comes home late, wet and sad. We hear him before we see him, the wet clop of Lassi's hooves, the sucking sound when he pulls them from the mud.

Father enters. He looks at the new mother seated at the dinner table, and, raising his eyebrows, motions with his head.

My twin holds the bread with the half-cherry pressed into it. Standing behind the rocking chair body, he stakes the bread onto the longest back slat. Mother has to have a head, after all.

We eat our simple meal quickly. We move to take the Mother outside, but Father stops us with a shake of his head.

Rain will ruin her.

The Mother has never stayed in the house. Today is a special day.

~

THE MOTHER SITS in the same place we left her a week ago. Father must stay near the tracks for another week. This happens often during rail work season. We chop wood, harvest carrots, potatoes, and turnips.

The Mother sits at the table. We set an empty plate for her every night, with a knife and fork. We don't know why.

Brother, did you hear that?
Hear what?
Sounded like a sigh.
Probably only the wind.

❧

TODAY WE GO OUT in the woods and forage for mushrooms. We bring back a basketful to dry for the winter months. We also bring back tree gum, as we have licorice root saved. We chew slowly, the bitter flavor spreading over our tongues. We like the texture because it feels like skin. We like the numbness that unfolds in our mouths, through our gums, as we work the root into the tree gum with our teeth and our tongues.

When Father returns, he frowns at The Mother being moved to the other side of the table.

I think my brother must have done it.

❧

FATHER WILL BE HOME for a few days. He helps us do the things we are not strong or skilled enough to do, like shoe Lassi or build a new roof for the henhouse. We are grateful we are two, and grateful for our father.

We make a stew that night, and Father watches how we prepare it, still convinced we will waste something even though for the past three years we have prepared every meal and know better. The Great Hunger Years left their mark on Father—he was our age when the famine began. Father will talk about the famine when he drinks, and when he does, his eyes empty and he does not see us or think of us anymore. He tells the story over and over. When he drinks he never stops talking, and the famine never stops hunting him.

We cut from the pine trees the pettu, *the husk of the tree, and we made bread with it. The sick and the old died first. My grandfather. Then the very young. My sister. Sometimes I wished to die in my sleep. We ate our horse. We boiled our belts and shoes. The only thing that kept the rest of us alive was living near the lake. We always had water. You should thank* Niinijärvi *every day for the water this lake gives you. Without her.*

He would start to come back to the room.

Without water. Without water.

If it was wintertime, he would leave and go to the sauna. We wouldn't see him again until morning.

But it is summer. So we sit in silence.

With a creak, The Mother begins rocking in place.

Creak

thump thud thump

creak

thump thud thump

We still say nothing.

Brother and I go up to bed. Father remains downstairs, talking quietly. My twin and I look at each other.

The creaking continues into the night.

FATHER WAKES BEFORE US. Or at least, he is awake when we wake. He has already made breakfast, and he's bathed as well. Smiling, he looks at us, waiting for something.

My twin and I exchange glances. We sit, nervous.

The Mother sits across from us, though really, she is always sitting.

Well, are you hungry or not?

We eat our eggs. Father still waits for something.

The Mother starts rocking. We realize what is different today.

The Mother has hair. A full head of hair. A dirty blond sort of hair, straight and long.

She wants it braided.

Mother, our real Mother, used to make *pulla*. Our favorite bread, made with cardamom. She would braid the dough after kneading, but "not too much, or the *pulla* will be hard," brushing it with egg on top, sprinkling it with cinnamon. We loved the feel of the velvety dough and the process of crushing cardamom with the mortar and pestle. The cardamom would release its perfume into the air, filling the cabin for two days, more if we were lucky.

We haven't made it for three years.

What are you waiting for? Our Father's cold voice brings us both back to the table. The Mother is rocking away, candied cherry lips glistening sticky and bright.

Brother and I slowly rise and go to The Mother. We each take half her hair, growing out of the loaf of bread, and begin to plait. Her hair reeks of caraway. Fine hair texture, but strong. I wonder what would happen if I pulled on her hair, not just pulled—ripped out a handful, plunged my hands into her head and screamed and screamed.

She too has a plate in front of her.

All the eggs have been eaten. A dirty fork sits on the edge of her plate.

We finish the braids and tie them off with a bit of red thread. Father seems pleased.

Brother and I say we must go to the lake today, that we are too dirty and have to clean ourselves and our clothes. We know we could bathe here, re-use the water to wash our clothes.

We want to wash the smell of caraway off our hands.

At the lake, brother and I sit, naked and shivering, together on the bank.

Silence covers the sky.

Brother?

(looks)

What is it?

Don't know. Hirviö.

Was it the two yolks?

Was it because we left it in the house?

Was it because I added caraway?

Was it because I forgot her face?

Was it because we forgot her face?

...Don't know.

We stay away from the house as long as we can. But the air turns too cold by the lake, even though the sun stays up, and we have to return.

Father is up with The Mother and dinner is made. They've already eaten.

≈

IN THE MORNING, I come down from our loft bed. We plan on doing our chores quickly and then going out to the woods to gather firewood. The Mother is still at the table. I can smell her hair and feel it between my fingers. I wipe my hands on my pajama pants.

Father leaves the house. Still in our pajamas, I sweep the cabin floor, while brother makes our bed upstairs. I open the door, and begin sweeping dirt and dead bugs out of the cabin.

A bird flies in.

A *Hömötiainen* flitters above with a "see-see see-see." These dainty black capped-birds. They stay in Finland year-round, never migrating. There is something so brave about the little black, grey and white birds. Their sharp, tiny black beaks, and bright black eyes. Determined eyes. Delicate birds, but unstoppable.

Captivated by the little bird, I leave the door open and four more fly in. They alight on our loft, then flit around the table, finally settling on the edge. They have our attention—my twin peers down from the loft. The five birds twitter to one another, their heads turning quickly this way and that, looking up and down.

The birds stop their chatter, turning their heads so one beady eye rests on The Mother. They begin to sway and hiss, as a snake hisses. They lunge as they hiss and spit, feigning striking with their beaks. One flies into her still, silent face, flapping violently and pecking at the hard bread.

The Mother's branch arms start moving, trying to keep the birds from attacking. She lets out something like a moan.

Father runs inside.

Protect your mother, protect her from the birds!

My brother and I do nothing.

Father grabs the broom from my hands and strikes at the birds, knocking one to the ground. The other four shriek, tiny and angry, and fly out the door.

The Mother moves her branch arms as though she is still being attacked. Twigs fall to the ground.

Father comforts The Mother, rubbing the pillow of her body and stroking her braids. When she stops waving her arms, he picks up the small bird from the floor. I haven't moved since the birds flew inside. My father stands in front of me, stone-faced.

Hold out your hands.

I make a cup with my palms and he drops the dead bird into it.

He looks up at the loft. My brother climbs down. Father points to the door.

We know what comes next. We don't recall what we did last time, but we remember this punishment.

We are locked in the sauna.

~

MY BROTHER and I cannot tell what day it is any longer; the sauna has no windows, only a small hole in the ceiling for the smoke to escape. A little light streams under the door.

We thought father would have let us out by now—but we also do not want to return to the cabin.

Drowned flies and gnats float in the water bucket, holding old, old water from the springtime rain. We drink it anyhow.

The dead bird is also with us. I don't know why I didn't drop it outside. Its small body, even lighter without life in it, lays on top of the birch woodpile, next to the stones. When my twin and I wake, we see it first.

Brother.

(looks)

We have to escape.

(nods)

Can we fit through the hole?

...Don't know.

We climb the short ladder to the covered hole and open the latch. It is a struggle, but we can fit. Wriggling out, we tumble down the roof and land breathless on the ground. It's night.

The moon illuminates everything.

We sneak to the house. We can't help ourselves.

Peering through the window, we see the back of The Mother. She's grown larger, the twigs which fell from her arms days earlier have grown back, and more in addition. Her pillow body looks filthy with earth, and the house is disastrous. There are piles of moss on plates, a moss feast. Dirt fills a few cups. Some are broken on the floor.

We see our Father standing behind The Mother, pushing into her. He wears nothing but his shirt and shoes.

We flee into the forest after gathering vegetables from the garden and fall asleep on the other side of the lake. We hold each other, shivering. The sky stares down on us.

For the next four days, we hide in the woods. We eat mushrooms and vegetables from the garden. We drink from the lake. We sleep on a bed of moss. We are grateful for each other and for our warm pajamas.

~

NIGHT FALLS SILENT AND CHILL. Brother and I steal to the cabin. The moon follows our path. We have what we need.

Father is sleeping on the floor. The Mother sits beside. The slats of the rocking chair are longer, the runners of the rocker thicker. Straw pokes out from her bursting pillow body. Littering the floor around her lay dead mice, missing their tails.

We stand in the doorway, waiting.

Waiting. Waiting.

She begins to stir, shaking her head and hair. She turns her head towards us, sensing the moss we carry. Can she smell it? Does she smell the damp earth? She reaches with her branch limbs.

She rocks, coming closer to us, looking with the holes in her face, the holes I made with my thumbs, her face that burned my thumbs. I can smell her caraway hair, I can taste it.

We turn and throw the moss in the direction of the sauna. She lets out a long, shrill whine and Father wakes.

We run.

Smoke plumes from the sauna. The smell of heat. Burning birch. Our hot, hot fire. Father runs to the sauna, and we follow. We stand on the south side of the sauna, and lock him inside.

The hatch is too small for him to fit through. We drank all the water.

Father bellows in the sauna, beating against the door. Time yawns and coils and crawls, twisting around my brother and me until we feel the heat in our stomachs rise. My brother takes my cold hand and tears run hot and silent.

A new scream comes. A howl charioted by many hostile scents. First acrid, then the scent of coal burning and then raw meat.

Meat and metal and sweet, we feel sick at how sweet the smell is. Putrid. Earth and bubbling fat.

Never touch burning logs, Father had said.

The Mother rocks out of the house with great care, taking many pauses. Her hair has come unplaited, and twists around the slats of her body in a tangled nest sprouting from her scalp. She leans forward and back, moving around the house grounds, sometimes using her arms, which have grown longer than my brother and I are tall, to steady herself or stop. Pausing in front of us, she rocks in place, pushing her branch limbs into the ground. Her unblinking eyes stare at us, and her mouth opens, decorated at the top and bottom by the candied cherry, now split in two. The hollow of her mouth deep and dark, we looked but could see neither its end nor its formation. No sound came from the space, and yet it was not silent. A yawning emptiness. An endless sky without stars, a bottomless well without water.

She turns away from us, and rocks with a creaking *thump thud thump thump thud thump* into the dark forest.

We stay outside the sauna as it burns, waiting. We stare into the sun as it rises.

Wine-Dark Eyes

Juniper White

THE FISHERMONKS RETURN from the sea on the Feast of Saint Miranda. They emerge from the mist over the moors, holding their writhing bouquets at their sides. It's always misty on the Feast of Saint Miranda, like the sea turns itself to sky just to clutch at the monk's robes.

I've never liked their bouquets. Wriggly bundles of fish and eels tied at the tail, clutched in the monks' water-worn hands. On the farm we use baskets and wheelbarrows and carts, but the fisher-monks carry their catch.

I watch them approach from my watch-spot in the dry grass. When I have free time, I come here to draw the tiny birds that stumble through the weeds on straw-thin legs. Today, though, my pencil lies listless against the blank page.

I spot Tomas amongst the marchers, scrawny but rigid. In her hand writhes a wrinkled octopus, tentacles tight around her wrist. Like the others, she stares straight ahead, clamoring barefoot over the rocks. They're all silent, their throats given over to the sea.

I slam my sketchbook shut, tuck my pencil in my skirts, and scurry down the dunes towards town. Jiddo tells me that seabirds never used to fly this far out. You'd have to trek out over the moors to see them, to where the fishermonks go, where the air turns to salt spray. But above me, a gull twists through the air, wings bent, its flight path a frenzied gyre.

~

I DIDN'T KNOW her well, I didn't. I saw her around, but I didn't know her. She was a year below me in school. I was preparing to work on Jiddo's farm and she was on track for the ocean, that daydream of seafoam washing over her irises. Before last Feast of Saint Miranda, I scarcely knew her name.

But there Tomas was at the fishermonks' reception. Jiddo doesn't make me stand with him while the monks line up to hand over their catch to the farmers. I always watch from within the crowd as the monks hand Jiddo their bouquets, flopping fish that only stop gasping when they leave the fishermonks' hands. I watch as long as I can and then I look away.

And when I looked away last Feast, there she was, clad in the sickly celadon robes of the fishermonks' order. Her hands were empty and her irises still fell into the black pool of her pupils; she was still an initiate. She saw me staring and tilted her head at me. I tilted back. And somehow, unspoken, we snuck off together and I found that her hands were as cold and clammy as they looked and that she was leaving for the sea tomorrow.

Today I watch as she stands with her fellow monks, stepping in unison. I watch as Jiddo and the rest of the council are handed fish after fish, more species than I could name, handed a full rainbow of eels, handed wriggling things with bulging eyes and jagged teeth, and then handed an octopus that stops squirming when Tomas lets go of it, dropping it into Jiddo's supplicant hands.

She returns to the robed mass and stares at nothing, and then I watch as she tilts her head to watch me.

~

THE FEAST of Saint Miranda is unlike any other feast, not just for the seafood. The monks drink and get drunk, some semblance of red returning to their washed-out flesh, wobbling when they walk, and they do it all in unsmiling silence. Their vomit is as clear as water and smells of brine.

I sit at Jiddo's table with the other farmhands, who all babble and gossip as well as they can; a few fishermonks have inexplicably elected to sit with us, and they stare over their mugs of ale. I pick at my sayadieh. Across the hall, Tomas sits with a school of monks, a bottle of wine in her hand, staring back at me.

I get up and make my excuses for leaving, apologizing away from my table, and meanwhile Tomas is just walking away from hers, enrobed in that fishermonk silence that justifies their every act. Then we're outside in the biting dark and it's just like it was last Feast, climbing onto the roof and helping each other up.

The mist obscures the sky, the black losing itself in haze. I try to find the constellations Tomas told me about last Feast, but they're lost in the clouds. Tomas's wine is made with blackberries and it tastes sweet and acrid on my tongue. I rest my pinky finger on tops of hers.

When I've heard enough of the music fading in from the Feast beneath us, when I've seen enough of the muted sky, I turn to look at her. She's already looking at me. I can still make out her pupils, faintly, but they can't contain all the saltwater foaming beneath her cornea.

Is this what you expected last Feast? I want to ask her. *How does it feel?* But I say nothing. She was marked from before we first spoke. Last Feast, she spoke of the ocean and her training, then spoke of stars and how the moon draws the tides like a far-away lover. She sang me hagiographies and whispered her fears, and when she said goodbye she said my name like it surprised her.

Tonight, I place my hand on her cheek and pry her lips apart with my thumb. She opens her mouth obediently. There, where her tongue should be, sits a white isopod, poking over her pearl teeth.

I don't speak either, just gaze into her mouth. The isopod looks at me with its wine-dark eyes, and so does she. I wonder if I could kiss her or if the ocean would snip off my tongue the second it touched her throat. Another gull dances drunk through the sky above us, wings twirling like a hurricane.

We Dwell in Its Many-Chambered Heart

A.C. Wise

ALANNA DIGS at the scant gap of light surrounding the door. The improvised tool in her hand is flat and white and worn. She found it in her pocket when she woke. She's fairly certain it used to be a bone.

Just as she's fairly certain she's tried this before, but it gives her something to do. It keeps her hands busy and her mind focused, not thinking of anything outside the walls. Not wondering if there's anything beyond the house at all.

Gouges mark the doorframe, the splintery, violent evidence of her previous attempts to leave. The door is painted blue today, but before it was forest green, claret red, unpainted but carved with pain-twisted faces rising like smoke. Today, the knob is dark brass and shaped like a sunflower. There are shiny patches where the patina has rubbed away. The petals dig into her palm when she grasps it. Sometimes, the knob is brushed stainless steel, other times, it is cut glass, sticky with fingerprints. All that remains unchanged is that it never turns all the way; it never sets her free.

Alanna rocks back on her heels, dragging an arm across her forehead, leaving streaks of dust or something worse behind. Her lower back aches from her awkward, crouched posture.

"It's not going to work, you know." Tom's voice filters into the hallway from the parlor.

She twists halfway around to look at him before she catches herself, annoyed. His tone is a goad, every line of his body designed to provoke with studied nonchalance. Legs kicked over the arm of a chair that was once plush velvet or expensive watered silk, now gone anemic and raw, washed to the dusty color of a moth's wing. He slumps bonelessly against the chair's high back while he turns pages that rustle like fallen leaves and look like dried skin.

The book's cover is nondescript. Plain black fabric faded to grey. No title visible, no author's name. Alanna can't see the pages from this angle, but she imagines them crinkled with old water stains and dense with spidery writing. The ink makes her think of brackish water, of dead things left to rot where they drowned.

Tom watches for her reaction, while trying to appear as though his attention is only on the page. The hearth behind him is unlit; the rest of the room is bare. Alanna rises, wiping her hands on her skirt, leaving behind smears the same dark shade as the ink in Tom's book.

She shouldn't take the bait, but she can't help herself. She stomps into the room, snatches the book from his hands and tosses it into the unlit hearth where the pages flutter like a downed bird.

"Why do you care what I do?" She looms over him, cheeks burning.

"I don't." Tom holds her gaze, knowing he's caught her, and between them, the air thrums.

The house yearns towards them, every wall, every floorboard thrilling to the promise of violence, like waiting for a breaking storm. How will it go this time? Alanna imagines throttling Tom, his neck stretching like taffy, flesh gone soft as dough as her fingers sink into him. Tom wants it as much as she does, as much as the house does, the glint in his eyes all but begging for the pain. Alanna practices breathing through her nose, but Tom's look still says he's won.

Today, he is Tom, but yesterday he was Randall. Just like today she is Alanna, and yesterday she was Sarah, or Niviah, Judith, or Dawn.

"I don't care at all." Tom says the words like a cat with feathers and bird bones crammed in its mouth.

He infuriates her. She loathes him. He's getting exactly what he wants from her, and even knowing as much, Alanna can't stop herself. She slaps him, the imprint of her hand burning a brand onto his cheek. Tom glances toward the cold hearth.

"You made me lose my page."

He unfolds, becomes a crooked column of shadow with unnatural proportions, head scraping the ceiling. An illusion, the house making him appear taller, allowing him to unsettle and intimidate her. He leans down, teeth a white sickle-cut in his face, breathing hot against her skin.

"I. Don't. Care." Alanna pronounces every word carefully, throwing his speech back at him.

She wonders what the house has done to her—given her eyes like lanterns, flesh like iron?

Tom continues to leer, and she punches him in the throat. He staggers back, accordioning into himself, making a choking sound. The house has a hold of them now; it won't let go until they're done.

Tom wheezes, granting Alanna a brief victory before he grabs her by the hair, drags her into the hall. Roots tear from her scalp and even amidst the pain, Alanna pictures thin filaments, tiny white threads burrowing miles underground. Fungal networks, extending miles, each fruiting body visible above ground only part of a larger, buried whole.

Tom slams her head against the wall and the image shatters as starbursts explode behind her eyes. Everything goes white and then grey, a stuttering lightning flash before her vision clears, leaving her skull ringing. At least there's the satisfaction of his skin scrunched beneath her nails, crimson beading on his wrist where she managed to dig in. They lurch into each other. Today, Tom is slightly faster. He catches her by the throat and Alanna's shoulder blades collide with the wall.

He turns her head, presses her cheek against the wallpaper, like he's trying to push her through the skin of the house itself. Alanna admires the pattern, taking a small, vicious joy in it even as Tom crushes her. Lining the hallway, the wallpaper is a muddy blue-green-grey, riotous with pale yellow-white chanterelles, wooly milkcaps, honey fungus, death caps. Mushrooms, dozens of varieties, more than she can name. She chuckles roughly, wishing the mushrooms were real, longing to break their soft bodies from the wood and cram them into Tom's mouth. Watching his veins flush blue-black with poison. Watching him choke.

Didn't that happen once before? It's hard to remember, hard to concentrate, especially when Alanna can't get enough air. Tom's fingers stray, sliding into her mouth, gagging her. She bites down. He screams. She kicks hard. There's a satisfying crunch. She spits blood on the floor—red that the wood drinks thirstily down.

The house likes it when they fight. Alanna pushes away from the wall feeling a pulse there under her fingertips—a contented echo of their rage. Or is it a shiver under the wood and plaster skin? Is the house stuck with them, trapped as they are?

Tom rakes at her face, going for her eyes. The swipe is clumsy. She whips her head to the side. The crescent where her teeth went into his flesh is angry, already bruising. Good. She hopes it turns infected.

He gets a grip on her wrist and slams it hard against the wall. Something cracks, something gives. In her wrist or the house itself. The surface yields. Tom pushes her through the wall, porous and spongy as mushroom skin. It envelops her, sucks her hungrily down, and she clings to Tom, determined to drag him with her.

This violence is familiar, intimate. She remembers it reframed, the frantic tearing of buttons, a different kind of desperate hunger driving them. Her skirts bunched in Tom's hands, his trousers shoved down by her own. Teeth nipping, just short of drawing blood. Another kind of grappling, but at the end of the day, the same need to dominate each other, to gain the upper hand.

Tom's eyes burn, bloodshot. He presses harder. More bones snap—hers and those of the house.

"I hate you," Tom says.

"I know," she responds.

She rams her head forward, slams it into his nose. He grins at her through the blood, undaunted, then clamps dull teeth on her throat. She thinks of pounds of pressure applied, the strength of a human bite. Their struggle becomes a death roll even as the house swallows them. They tumble through the dark, digested.

Everything will reset, as it always does. They will wake and start all over again.

∾

ALANNA BLINKS, lying on the floor of one of the bedrooms. Shouldn't she be Alexandra today? Or Tiffany? Or Roxanne?

But no, she's Alanna today and she was Alanna yesterday. Does that mean anything? Is it a good sign, or a bad one?

Minute, gritty particles filter down from the ceiling as though someone paces back and forth above. She's on the second floor. Overhead is the attic. There's a freestanding mirror; Tom smashed her face into it once when she was Eloise and he was Daniel. Or maybe it was the other way around. There's a dress form and a massive sea chest; she locked him inside it when he was Timothy and she was Victorine. She sat on the lid, kicking her heels against its side and delighting in his hoarsening voice, his fading screams.

Dust lands on her cheeks. She doesn't have the energy to wipe it away. Everything hurts.

Lying on the floor, Alanna catalogues the house. The entryway, with the door that never opens. The dining room and parlor to the left, the library with its empty shelves to the right—like a carcass stripped bare. The kitchen, the conservatory. Upstairs, the bedrooms—one that looks like it was meant to be a nursery at one time, another repurposed as a study. The attic above that. They've crawled through every inch of the house a dozen times over, tried every window, every chimney, every door, looking for a way out.

They haven't been in the basement since…

Alanna fists her hands into the fabric of her skirts and feels the outline of something hard in her pocket, centering and oddly soothing. She focuses on her breathing, on the room around her instead. The walls are papered in pale blue. Patches have been ripped away, revealing crusted scabs of adhesive underneath. Molded features decorate the ceiling, threads of actual mold winding between them.

The mold moves. It twitches, blooms and swirls, painting a magic lantern show across the whiteness that makes Alanna's breath catch in her throat. The silhouettes are familiar. It's her and Tom—except they were Stephen and Armand, or Greyson and Annabelle, Virginia and Suzanne back then. They travelled in a carriage through the countryside. A wheel broke. They ran to the house for shelter from a storm. It never let them out again.

They were co-workers on a business trip. Their car broke

down. They were having an inappropriate workplace affair. The house punished them for their sins.

They were strangers. They'd never met until the moment Tom's car fishtailed into hers on the rain-washed road. Neither of them had a signal on their phones, but they could see the house in the distance and made the dash with their coats held over their heads to see if someone in there would call for a tow.

They knew each other far too well—siblings, twins, come to the house to fight over their grandmother's inheritance. Squabbling like carrion crows, their grandmother not even yet a corpse. They were thieves and then murderers when things went too far.

They weren't quite siblings, but they were family still. Tom was married to Alanna's sister. They hated each other with a fiery passion, but after a night of drinking from a dusty bottle rescued from the back of a cupboard, all their contempt and disgust for each other boiled over into something else. They broke her sister's heart and she's been haunting them ever since.

Every one of these pasts is true. The mold curling across the ceiling does not lie. She has been all of these things and will be again.

Alanna's fingertips tingle with the memory of threading through Tom's hair. It's as familiar to her as the feeling of pressing down on his eyelids while he sleeps, not giving up until something pops. His lips against the skin of her throat and the feel of his teeth there instead. Her skirts rucked up around her waist, their hipbones bruising against one another, his body pinning hers to the wall, and the house pulling them both in.

The shadow play continues unspooling. They've never been anywhere other than here. The house birthed them, fruiting bodies extruded from its walls. Puppet things, tethered by long, fungal strands, moved like players on a stage.

Dust trickles from the corners of her eyes like gritty tears. She imagines Tom pacing around up there, worrying at their past like a bone. She imagines the ghosts of her former selves, a thousand murdered Alannas, treading across the boards.

She exhales, and the house exhales with her. Alanna climbs to her feet, brushing off dust, wishing she could brush off the layers of bruising and scars as well. She doesn't want to fight, she never does. But her hand slips into her pocket as she descends the stairs.

The bone has grown so thin that it's sharp when she tests its edge against her thumb.

Tom sits at the head of the long table in the dining room. The walls here are the color of liver and blood. The chandelier overhead is festooned with cobwebs. The dish in front of him is empty. He stares at the wall.

He doesn't look up until she's right beside him, resting a hand on his shoulder. He wears a morning coat, as ridiculously old fashioned as her layers of skirts. The expression that meets hers is forlorn, the skin around his eyes dark with lack of sleep, his lids glazed with tears.

"I'm sorry," Tom says; it sounds sincere.

She can't bear it, that he is the first to crack, the first to apologize.

Alanna says, "Me too."

She draws the bone like a straight razor across his throat. Blood fountains into the empty dish in front of him, a hot, salty, bitter soup. Tom slumps forward, and Alanna leaves him facedown. She takes the chair at the other end of the table. She folds her arms into a pillow, rests her head atop them. She will wait right here until the house resets again, until this horrid day ends.

ALANNA STUDIES THE WORN BONE, turning it in her hand. The name Alanna seems to be sticking. Does that mean it belongs to her, or has she grown too weary, too lazy to come up with a new one?

She shouldn't have killed Tom and left him cooling in his own blood. They've slaughtered each other countless times, but it never stops being unkind.

"We could try working together," she says.

The house thrums, shivering around her. In response to her words, or something else? Is the house eager for them to leave? All the times they've slaughtered each other, has the house been rooting for a different outcome? Will it be proud when they finally work it out, or is it simply setting them up to fail again? Giving them hope to make it all the sweeter when it's snatched away.

The walls in the conservatory are papered in dark plum,

flocked with a lattice pattern in gold. The color of a bruise, over-laid with pale, creeping rot. The only furniture is a piano between her and a fireplace large enough that if she stooped to enter, she could fully stand inside. Alanna knows she could fit in the fireplace, because she did so once upon a time, scrambling up into the chimney to hide from Tom. Wedged there, suffocating in the terrible dark with his laughter echoing in her ears.

Tom crouches beneath the piano, knees pressed against his chest, arms wrapped over his head as if fearing a blow. Heavy, mildewed curtains hang over bay windows, blocking out the light.

"I'm tired of fighting," Alanna says. "I'm going into the basement."

She doesn't ask him to come with her; she won't stop him if he follows. She tucks the bone into her pocket. The train of her skirt drags over the floorboards, etching arcane symbols in the dust. The piano bench scrapes back, allowing Tom to crawl out. She doesn't look behind her, she can imagine him well enough, following her, looking meek and contrite.

The kitchen is yellow—like turned butter, like a tooth clinging to a weathered skull. There's a door—massive, wooden, heavy. Alanna hauls the bar aside, drops it to the kitchen floor. The stairway unfurls when the door is opened, a throat smelling of dirt, inviting them into the dark. There's no switch or pull cord, no tap to turn to raise fluttering gas flames. Just shadows massed where the wooden steps end.

There's a box of matches in her pocket alongside the bone. Tom presses a candle into her hand without being asked—slick yellow-white wax like rendered fat. She hands him the box of matches once she's done, hears the rough strike as he lights a candle of his own.

Shadows waver, but the light falls only in a scant circle, failing to illuminate more than a few steps at a time. The warm wax smell pushes the smell of earth back, but not far enough. It's still there, haunting the edges of the light. Alanna takes the first tentative step. Tom could push her from behind, send her tumbling like a broken doll. The boards creak, Tom following her down.

Grit crunches under her boots. The floor gives way to packed earth as they cross the basement, Tom crowded close enough for her to feel the panicked beat of his heart. There's a waist-high trough of stone, wider than her outstretched arms and at least twice as long. It's filled with black earth. White bones peek out from the loamy dark. Not a trough, but a grave.

Dirt fills the eye sockets and mouth of a skull, jaw wrenched open in an endless scream. Alanna can't decide if the earth is rejecting the bones, forcing the skeleton up and out, or whether it's in the process of being swallowed whole.

A rib has been snapped uncleanly away where it arcs out of the dirt, leaving a jagged stump behind. Alanna strokes a finger over the bone tucked into her pocket, then withdraws her finger to touch it to the plane of a cheekbone instead.

This is their grandmother, the one whose inheritance drove them to murder. This is her sister, whose heart they broke.

This is her; the bones are Alanna's own.

She remembers being buried here, and the stone trough is wide enough to accommodate two of them, side by side. She remembers clawing her way free, mushroom hardening into a skeleton, into skin as the earth spit her unmercifully to the ground. She clung to the stone to pull herself upright, shuddering, flesh goose-pimpled, coughing up soil. She took Tom's hand to help him free. He slapped her away, pushed her down. They took their fear out on each other for the first, but not the last time.

"Do you…" she asks, turning to face Tom.

His eyes are luminous in the dark. She knows exactly how his cheek would bruise under the impact of her fist; she tangles her fingers into the fabric of her skirt instead. He nods, remembering all the same histories she does, countless lives spent between these rotting walls.

The house is punishing them; it's teaching them how to live. They are its spores, waiting to be released into the world.

Alanna turns, shadows dragging across the floor until the circle of light falls on a square iron trap set flush with the ground. There's a ring. There's no lock that she can see. It looks heavy enough that it will take both of them to lift it.

Filaments of white, threads woven underground. A network stretching miles through the dark. She sets her candle on the floor, glances over her shoulder at Tom.

Will it end as always, the two of them scrambling over each other like rats in the dark? Her nails breaking and ripping free from their beds as she digs wildly at the earth. Tom grabbing her heel, dragging her backward. The house tightening its leash, pulling them both back into its heart again.

She takes Tom's hand. His fingers twitch against hers; she has shattered those fingers a thousand times. Alanna skates the fingers of her other hand across his cheek. She could dig her nails in and he would respond by snapping her neck. By kicking her in the stomach, stamping on her ribs until one of them broke and punctured a lung, drowning her in blood.

Alanna leans her head forward until it touches his. Tom's breath warms her skin.

"I'm afraid," she says.

Admitting the words aloud hurts worse than the most painful of her deaths; she might as well bare her throat, tell him he's won, but Tom doesn't move.

"I don't know if this will work," she says. "But I'm going to try."

She imagines him crawling behind her in the dark, shoving her face down into the dirt so she can't breathe. She imagines kicking out as hard as she can with him on her heels, cratering his face into a hole of blood.

Like his fingers, Tom's mouth is cold. It tastes like dirt. She doesn't stop kissing him. Lover, sibling, stranger, enemy, friend.

Alanna steps back, lets go of his hand. She bends and grasps the ring and together they open the door. She speaks without looking at him.

"Follow me into the dark."

Dark Water

Andrew Humphrey

IN LATE AUTUMN cormorants gather on the roof of the old mill that sits opposite my flat. I see them on my early morning walks, stark against an austere sky. Eventually, they peel off, one by one, dropping and diving, skimming sleek and flat, parallel to the surface of the narrow river that runs between my home and the mill.

I moved here less than a year ago, after Mary, my wife of almost forty years, died in an accident; a stupid, random thing. Everything moved too quickly following her death; the funeral, the house move, all the grinding admin that bereavement brings, sliding by in a grainy blur. I had my daughter, Grace, to guide me through it, which was both a blessing and a curse. She is a brisk, practical girl—woman, I suppose—and she appeared to relish the dull, grey sequence of forms and meetings and telephone calls that unfurled in their own monotonous rhythm. When they were done and her mother was finally, irrevocably gone, Grace seemed lost momentarily. I remember her after the wake, adrift in the middle of a rapidly emptying pub carpark, fixed in a single lampposts sodium haze. She has a melancholy air, even in her better moments, and then especially so, with her head bowed and her large, downcast eyes beginning to shimmer with tears.

I'd had a drink or two more than I should have, I suppose—it was my wife's funeral, after all—and I was growing impatient in the chilly air. "Now, now, Grace. What would your mother say."

She blinked slowly—Grace does everything slowly—and looked at me. "She might have wondered why *you* didn't cry, Dad."

I ushered her towards the car. "It's a generational thing. I don't expect you to understand."

~

As well as the cormorants, I often encounter Steven during my morning walks. I prefer the cormorants. Steven is also a widower. There are a few of us here, in this discrete outcrop of properties designed for the elderly and the alone. He is a little older than me, I think, although he wears it well.

I see him now, hands in pockets, stood on the pavement by the river's edge. We are close to my flat. I can still see the cormorants from here. I find it a comfort, knowing that they are there. I have no idea why.

Steven's head dips towards me as I approach. "You'll never guess what I saw last night," he says, by way of greeting. His voice is light and cheerful. He is smiling. He is always like this. A single swan drifts down the centre of the river, heading towards the narrow bridge that lies to our left.

"If I will never guess, you may as well tell me."

He ignores the sourness in my voice, as he always does. "Otters! A pair of them, right outside my bedroom window."

I am surprised, although I do not want to show it. "What about that."

"They woke me. Mating, I suppose. Hell of a racket, sounded like they were killing each other. It was before five and there was no more sleep for me after that, but it was worth it. Otters! Half a mile from the city centre."

"We're not exactly short of wildlife here." This is true, up to a point; squirrels, pike in the river, rats, of course, the occasional fox. Egyptian geese, haughty and raucous. Still … I liked otters. I wished that I had seen them. "You didn't think to take a photo, I suppose?"

"Didn't have time, old boy." Old boy. Christ, I hate that. "And I was half-asleep. Not at my sharpest."

"Perhaps you dreamt it, Steven."

His laugh is warm and genuine. He wears a velvet jacket and a crimson cravat. He wouldn't look out of place in a cocktail bar. It is seven-thirty in the morning. "It was no dream." He pulls a tissue from a trouser pocket and gives his nose a languorous blow. His face is typically open and friendly as he turns to me. "Fancy a coffee? That place around the corner is open shortly. Or you could come to mine?"

"Love too. But I'm seeing Grace today. Need to tidy up a bit. She'll only nag if I don't."

"Another time, then," he says, his hand resting on my shoulder.

"Another time," I say, easing past him.

~

"THIS PLACE IS A TIP," Grace says, fussing around me, picking up plates and cups and folding newspapers. Of course it is. I know if I leave my housework for long enough, Grace will do it for me.

She makes tea and we settle in the small living area. These places are artfully designed; all ground floor, easy access, warm and compact and suffocating.

I tell her about Steven and his precious otters. "I don't know why you are so hard on him. He seemed perfectly pleasant to me." We'd bumped into him once, Grace and I, just as she was leaving my apartment. He'd been charming. Of course he had, it came so easily, it was like breathing to him.

"He won't take a hint. Keeps asking me for a coffee."

"Perhaps he likes you."

"Unlikely. I don't give him the slightest encouragement."

She shrugs slowly. "Perhaps he's just a nice man. Maybe he thinks that you are lonely."

"Lonely? What if I am? What business is it of his?"

Her head turns towards mine. Her thick fingers are steepled together in her lap. "And are you?"

"Am I what?"

"Lonely?"

I love my daughter. Of course I do. But, sometimes....

Mary named her Grace. Even as a baby, it was clearly a ridiculous name; she was too big, too ponderous. Nothing like her mother at all.

"Of course I'm lonely." I'm aware of the bitterness in my voice. It seems to run through me continually these days; perhaps it has for years. Maybe I'm simply waiting for the poison to drain.

She looks at me and waits and drinks her tea. When it's clear that I have no more to add, she says, "Perhaps he's gay."

"What? Who?"

"Steven, of course."

"Steven, gay? But he was married. He had a wife." I used to be an editor, so I am instantly aware of the redundancy. It irritates the hell out of me.

"Yes. I know. Still … perhaps he fancies you, Dad."

After a moment, I say, "I know you're joking, Grace. It isn't very funny."

She drinks some more tea, eats a shortbread biscuit, and then another. "Amy is fine, thanks for asking."

"I was just about to…"

"She's busy, of course. Her school are making cuts, so it isn't easy."

"Well, it can't be. Not with all those holidays she has."

She sighs and places her cup carefully back onto the saucer. "I love you, Dad."

I don't know what to say to that, so I stand and walk into the kitchen. From the window I can see across the river. Two cormorants are perched on the roof of the building opposite. The sight of them causes my breathing to ease. I see a small figure scuttle across the pavement towards the river and I adjust my focus in order to track it. I start to say something.

Grace joins me. Her breath is warm on my face. "It's a cat," she says.

"I know it's a cat."

"You thought it was one of Steven's otters, didn't you?"

I'm not sure what annoys me more; her instant appraisal of my assumption or the implication that the otters somehow belong to Steven. "It's daylight, Grace. So it would be unlikely."

She pats my shoulder gently and makes her way back into the living room.

"I read this sentence once; in a novel, when I was editing."

"Okay," she says, turning, frowning, pulling at the too-long sleeves of her cardigan.

"The writer described a female character as "otter-sleek and beautiful.""

"I don't like that much." Grace writes poetry, so she thinks that she understands these things.

"Neither did I. I cut it, of course."

"Are you okay, Dad?"

"The thing is, that same evening, we were attending this black tie dinner. Your mother came down the stairs, late as usual. She wore this long velvet dress. Her hair was jet black then, and it fell to her shoulders. Everything about her was frictionless. For a moment I could neither breathe nor speak. She looked…."

"Otter-sleek and beautiful?"

"Yes."

"You still cut it, though? The sentence?"

"Of course I did." The air between us has changed. I shrug. "This was years ago. When your mother still had her figure. Before…" I hesitate.

"Before she had me."

"I didn't say that."

Grace turns her back to me and starts to clear up the tea things.

~

THAT NIGHT I see the shape for the first time.

I am pulled awake a little before three. Perhaps it was a dream that woke me, although if it was, all trace of it fled instantly. Maybe it was a noise from outside; Steven's otters, possibly, although it would more likely be rats, or a cat, hunting them.

It has been this way since Mary died. Sometimes I'll doze for an hour or two longer, some nights I barely sleep at all.

Now, I rise and dress quickly and step out into a still, cold night. The sight of the river calms me. I walk along the cobbles and the pathway at the water's edge, past the slipway, towards the bridge that leads to the city centre.

When I stop I am close to Steven's flat. I gaze at the river's surface and wait for my mind to still. It can be hypnotic, the gentle ripple of the tiny wavelets, silver-edged beneath a lurking moon. I suppose I want an otter to appear; I imagine telling Steven and pricking his smug little bubble of self-satisfaction. Even as the thought forms, I know it to be incorrect; he would be pleased for me. He would be warm and happy. He might even mean it. The bastard.

Just then the surface of the water moves, and for a moment, I think that it *is* Steven's otter, but I soon realise that I am wrong. This shape is too big. It is vague and formless and although it threatens to break the surface of the river, it never quite does. It moves in languid, erratic circles. Water laps around it, moonlight breaks along its contours. I frown and concentrate, but still I cannot tell what it is. It is nothing human, I assume, though people have been known to swim along this stretch of river, or not obviously human, at least. I am curious, rather than frightened. When the shape disappears there are no bubbles, no trail in the water, no sign that anything was there at all.

In the morning I assume that I imagined it.

~

ALTHOUGH I AM past retirement age, I still work a little. Freelance editing, proofreading, some typesetting on occasion. I work from home, I never have to meet anyone face-to face, which is just as well. Mary smoothed off my rough edges. Now I think I consist only of edges and sharp angles.

I enjoy the work, although it is slumming it, compared to what I was used to; Chief commissioning editor at a major publisher. Oh, you would have heard of them. I was good. Mary was drawn to me then. And you had to be a bit of a bastard in those days, if you wanted to get anywhere. Which I did. So did Mary, although she denied it later.

She was my secretary and then my assistant and then much more than that. It was our material success which enabled us to buy our dream cottage close to Holt—15th century, thatched, compellingly beautiful and deeply, stupidly impractical.

Grace took one look at the steep, narrow staircase that led up to the second floor and called it a death trap. I dismissed her curtly, I recall. Even Mary laughed the comment off.

It turned out that this time, Grace was right.

~

IT IS ALMOST a week before I see Steven again. As usual he greets me with an instant, assumed bonhomie. "David! How good to see you. She really is lovely, isn't she?"

I am thrown; by his words, by his warmth, by the ridiculously over-sized, fluffy, multi-coloured scarf that he wears, wrapped multiple times around his slender, elegant throat. "What? Who?"

"Grace."

"Grace? When did you see my daughter?"

His smile falters for a moment. "The day before yesterday. She was with her beautiful wife. I assumed that they were visiting you?"

"Ah. I remember now. They dropped in, but I missed them. An appointment. Such a shame."

"Well, I'm sure you will catch up soon. She's a credit to you, I must say. And your late wife, of course."

"She is?"

"She's adorable, David! That smile. She's so genuine…if we'd ever been blessed with children, I would…" He hesitates and looks at the pavement and then at me, again. "Sorry. I get a bit carried away sometimes."

Just a bit, I think. And is this my Grace, he is talking about? Perhaps I have another daughter, one who *is* adorable and…I realise that he is staring at me, waiting for me to speak. "Yes. Takes after her mother, I suppose. Was she well?"

"Yes." Another hesitation. "It's very sad about Amy's mother."

"Her mother?"

"That bloody illness. It's what took my Judy, of course." He shakes his head. We move aside to let a small family of Egyptian geese shuffle past; the parents are wary and watch us constantly as their offspring bumble on and off the pavement. "She's a fighter, though, by all accounts, so one must hope, mustn't one?" Must one, I think? But I merely nod. Another pause. When he speaks he avoids eye contact, which is unusual for Steven. "I think she's worried about you, old boy."

"Worried?"

"Look, I know it isn't my place, but ..." He is struggling now and I find that I am enjoying it. "Your wife..."

"I beg your pardon?" This is definitely and spectacularly *not* his place.

"Grace's mother."

"That's how these things generally work."

He looks directly at me now. His face is more lined than I remember. His expression is one of such deep empathy, that I suddenly want to push him into the river. "The accident ... Grace is worried that you might blame yourself. She thinks that you are carrying this enormous burden of guilt. And that explains ..."

Another pause. "Explains what, Steven?"

"Look, I've said too ..."

"It was a long chat you had, Steven? With my daughter and her wife?"

"Yes. They came in for coffee. She just needed to talk, I think."

"Did she?"

"I hope I haven't...."

"She thinks that you might be gay, you know."

His expression clears completely and for a moment I think I might have broken through his veneer of smug complacency. Then his head twists backwards and he gives a laugh so loud and hearty that it startles a group of nearby pigeons into sudden flight. "Yes! She told me. So funny. And your reaction. Priceless."

"Oh."

"But perhaps she is right, David." He places a hand on my shoulder. "Perhaps I do fancy you. This is all a ruse, I am trying to...."

"Don't be ridiculous."

He withdraws his hand. "I'm sorry."

He doesn't look sorry. "Why do you persist in this?"

"In what?"

"Speaking to me. Acting as though we are friends?"

"I'm just being sociable. It's in my nature."

"It's more than that."

He shrugs. "You puzzle me. You seem to dislike me so. I am nothing but friendly and...I am curious, I suppose."

"I do not like you, Steven."

"Why not?"

"Oh, that's easy. My wife had a lover and he looked exactly like you."

"What? That's…that isn't my fault."

"It's not your fault at all. But…there it is. When I see you, I see James. When I see James, I see Mary. With James."

"Goodness. I'm sorry."

"No need to apologise. Nothing you can do about it."

He gives a wrinkly grin. "There's plastic surgery, I suppose."

To my surprise, I laugh. It sounds odd. "Well, if you wouldn't mind. Old boy."

I match Steven's dry chuckle with one of my own. He reaches out a hand and, after a moment, I shake it.

The silence that follows is almost companionable. "See you around," he says eventually. He smacks his hands together and turns towards the direction of his flat.

I watch him as he walks away. "I didn't kill my wife," I say to his retreating back. I am not sure if he hears me.

When I glance at the old mill, the cormorants have gone.

NOVEMBER IS DYING. It is quiet and dull and not putting up much of a fight. I dread December and all of its attendant horrors. The Christmas adverts have started already and the most awful music is piped into the supermarkets on a continual loop.

I see the shape twice more before the month ends; once in the early hours, once at dusk, both times in different stretches of the river. I cannot quite make out what it is. It always threatens to break the surface of the water, but it never does. The light is tricky here, the moonlight intermittent, my eyesight not strong enough to trust what I see. Is it getting larger? Are those shoulders surging up against the oil-dark water? If they *are* shoulders, where is the head?

By the time the latest sighting ended, dusk was edging into full night. It was dry, had been for days, and a low mist lingered. As I walked back towards my flat, I heard footsteps behind me. They sounded wet, as though whomever was causing them, was utterly water-logged. When I stopped walking, the footsteps stopped. When I turned, there was nobody there.

～

WHEN I NEXT SEE GRACE SHE tells me that her and Amy are moving to Japan. I assume initially that she means for a holiday, but she soon dispels that idea.

"We're going there to live, Dad."

"Oh." We're standing on the bridge from which there is a view of my flat and of the old mill. A pair of black-headed gulls perch where the cormorants are usually to be found. I resent the sight of them and I am glad when they finally fly away. "You must have been planning this for months?"

"Yes."

"You didn't think to mention it to me?"

"We didn't think that you would care."

"Of course I care." But the hesitation, the tone of my voice... Grace does not respond.

We gaze at the water. I will the shape to appear so that I can show Grace, ask what she thinks it might be; but, of course, it does not.

As we walk, though, I hear a sound from directly behind me. I stop abruptly. Grace says, "What?"

"Did you hear that? Behind us?"

"I didn't hear anything."

"Footsteps. Wet footsteps. They were very loud, you must have...."

"I didn't hear anything, Dad." She looks at me, her expression one of irritation, rather than concern. "Are you okay? I suppose we could delay...."

"No. Goodness, no. I'm fine. Don't go changing your plans for me. I wouldn't want to put you out."

She walks on, her back to me. When I follow, there is only silence behind me.

～

THAT NIGHT I dream of the shape and of the wet footsteps. In the dream, something has sloughed itself landward and is waiting by my door. River-water drips methodically onto my doorstep. Something squelches wetly against the handle and I hear it turn.

When I wake I am screaming Mary's name, in a voice that is thin and weak and not entirely my own.

~

THE FIRST DAY in December I meet Steven for coffee at a nearby Italian deli. It is snug and warm. The scent of dried meats and strong cheeses forms a genial fog. There are panettone, of course, and other festive arrangements, but one can't have everything.

We sit opposite each other. The coffee is strong and good. I tell him about Grace and her plans. His hesitation informs me that he already knows. "I'm sorry. I bumped into her again, after she left you."

"Of course you did."

"It's such exciting news, though, isn't it? Japan! What a wonderful country. I have always been fascinated...."

"Yes. Me too."

"Really? Well, that's where she gets it from, then?"

"Perhaps. She has visited often. Amy has family there."

He pauses a moment. It is clear that he knows this also. "I suppose that now Amy's mother has gone...."

"Gone?"

He is incredulous. "She died. Surely Grace told you this?"

"To be fair, I didn't ask."

"Oh, Steven...."

"Look, we are all but estranged, Grace and I. We were never close, and since her mother died...well, it's difficult. *I'm* difficult, I suppose is the truth of it." I wait for him to contradict me, but he doesn't. Instead, his attention is drawn towards the counter, where a dark-haired woman is serving slices of pizza to a bright young couple. "Did she say anything else?" Steven looks back at me, his expression querulous. "Grace? When you bumped into her?"

"Yes, in fact she did." I wait for him to continue. He sips his coffee. "She asked if I would keep an eye on you."

"What?"

"Now that we are such firm friends."

"We are not friends, Steven."

"Of course we're not. Still." He drains his cup. "She thinks you might be losing it. Says that you are hearing things."

"What nonsense."

"That's what I thought. But…" He shrugs as he stands and makes his way to the counter to order more coffee. I watch him. Does he really look like James? His mannerisms, perhaps. His charm. It occurs to me, though, that almost every male face I see reminds me, in some way, of that deceitful bastard.

He sits, frowns. "Where were we?"

"Do you ever see things, Steven? In the river?"

"Of course I do. Perch. Tench. The occasional shopping trolley when the water is low."

"That's not what I mean."

"Tell me, then." So I do, briskly, economically, just as a good editor should. He listens with his fingers steepled beneath his chin. When I am finished, he says, "Have you been drinking, David?"

"I haven't had a drink since Mary died."

"I see."

"Do you think Grace has a point? I must say, I am beginning to wonder."

"You were drunk? When…the accident happened?"

"Grace been filling you in, has she?"

He twists awkwardly in his seat. "I think she just needed to…."

"To talk. I know. Yes, I was drunk. Mary was drunk. That's why she fell down the stairs. I doubt that she would have done so, were she sober."

"And you…."

"Blacked out. Old boy. First I knew of it was when I woke in the night and found her. Sobered me right up, I must say. She was still beautiful, though. Even at her age. Even in death."

"At her age?"

"We'd had a row. That was the pattern, then; drinks and a shouting match. About James, of course. Always about James." I look into my coffee, wishing it were whisky, a good one; although I suppose that blended would do. "Eight years it went on. I never knew. He was my friend, best man at our wedding. I never had a clue. She only told me after he died."

"James is dead?"

"Yes."

"How did he die?"

"He drowned. He had a boat, on the broads. Damn fool fell in. Couldn't swim, so that was that."

"Another accident."

"Another accident."

He gives a weak grin. "They seem to follow you around. Perhaps I should watch myself."

"Perhaps you should." The grin fades. "That was a joke, Steven."

"Of course. Very funny."

"Footsteps. That's what I heard, when I was with Grace. Wet footsteps, echoing right behind me. I hear them when I am alone too. Almost every time I walk I hear them. When I turn, there is nobody there."

"Wet footsteps?"

"Yes."

"We have had no rain."

"I know."

"Look, David, all of this trauma; it's not surprising that you are seeing things, hearing things."

I shrug. "James died. Mary died. The trauma was theirs, not mine."

"I'm not sure it works like that. Have you considered…."

"Seeking help?"

He notes my tone. "Well, yes. Counselling. Therapy. There's no shame in it."

"Isn't there?"

He sighs. "David…you are aware of what century we inhabit, I assume?"

I offer a tiny smile. I realise, that for once, I do not want to argue. "Sadly, yes. Look, it's just not for me, that's all. I can't see that talking changes anything. Things happen; good things, bad things. Either way, they pass. As this will pass. All this weird stuff."

"Some would call you a Stoic, David."

"I have been called much, much worse."

He grunts and folds one leg across the other, tugging the crease in his trousers straight in the same motion. "Anyway. Christmas is around the corner. Any plans?"

"Nice subject change. Very subtle."

"I didn't mean…."

I place a hand on his arm and he appears startled by the contact. "It doesn't matter, Steven. I find, as the years pass, that very little *actually* matters."

"I cannot agree." I shoot him a look of mock astonishment. He grins at that, as do I, and the air around us settles as we return to more comfortable ground. "It is possible that I am a fraction less cynical than you. Old boy."

"On reflection, I think that might well be the case."

We drink our coffee in a brief, companionable silence. Steven says, "This shape that you see? Could it be one of my otters, perhaps?"

"Unlikely. Unless it's a giant otter and it has no head."

"Oh."

"No more sightings, I assume?"

"Sadly, no. Perhaps *I* am imagining things."

"I doubt it. If you say that you saw otters, I am sure that you did." He appears rendered speechless by the apparent compliment. "I miss the cormorants, though."

He frowns deeply. "What do you mean?"

"I would have thought that sentence was self-explanatory." I repeat it slowly, as one would to a child.

"But they are there; every morning. I see them as our sentinels. I feel that they are watching over us, keeping us safe."

"That's odd," I say, pushing my coffee cup to one side. "I haven't seen them for days."

~

CHRISTMAS APPROACHES, but the cormorants do not return; not for me, at least. The shape haunts me, as do the damp, slow footsteps, which dog me every time I leave the flat. They match my pace precisely. They cease when I cease. There is nothing there when I turn. I am still drawn to the river, though, at dusk, at night. I cannot resist the lure of it.

My sleep is shredded. The dreams grow worse. In the latest I sense the cold, wet presence at my bedroom door. I see the handle begin to turn. When I wake, my mouth is wide open, but I am making no noise at all.

~

GRACE'S TRAVEL plans are far advanced and she is too busy to see me over Christmas. Steven is visiting family in Exeter. He leaves on Christmas Eve, and we squeeze in a last coffee before he catches his coach. He tells me that he has read up on cormorants (because, of course he has) and that they represent the need for a sense of purpose. He wonders if this is what I need, what I lack. I pretend that I have no idea what he is talking about.

As he leaves, I realise that I will miss him. We shake hands and he turns and as I watch his back recede into the distance, I feel a weird, hot prickling sensation behind my eyes.

I soon put a stop to that.

~

I WAKE at three the next morning, attempting to scream. When the terror has settled I rise and dress.

"Happy Christmas," I say, to nobody in particular.

I walk by the river, because what else is there for me to do?

The night is cold and still. A low mist drifts across the water. I watch the surface as I walk, waiting for the shape to appear, wanting to get it over with. I visit both bridges and the long, straight stretch that leads towards the city centre, but the river remains undisturbed.

It takes me sometime to register that the footsteps have disappeared also. I walk for another half an hour, varying my pace, stopping occasionally to look behind me. There is only silence and an empty path.

I am tired and cold by the time I circle back to my home. The flat will be warm. Perhaps Christmas Day is a good a day as any to start drinking again.

As I approach my flat I glance upwards, but the cormorants have not returned.

When I open my front door, for a moment the interior is lit by moonlight; just a little, just enough. I cannot comprehend what it is that I see in front of me. I am grateful when the clouds close again, and all is dark.

Foreword to 'Occult Methods of Investigation'

David Peak

WELCOME to the thirteenth edition of *Occult Methods of Investigation*.

You're reading this because you want to know more. It's only human, after all, to want to go *deeper*, to learn more about *what it all means*. And in this way, the question of *why* people do the things they do, as terrible as they often are, is one of the fundamental questions of human existence. This textbook provides an introduction to conducting such inquiries via the medium of criminal investigation.

What attracts someone to studying the darker sides of human behavior? Perhaps it's the need to better understand ourselves and what we are capable of, those things that polite society deems unthinkable. Still, the clues related to each and every criminal case must lead *somewhere*, to some destination, and although this destination cannot be predicted or controlled, it can be imagined, intuited, and supported by evidence both material and immaterial.

As Poe writes in "The Murders in the Rue Morgue:" "Between ingenuity and the analytic ability there exists a difference far greater, indeed, than that between the fancy and the imagination, but of a character very strictly analogous. It will be found, in fact, that the ingenious are always fanciful, and the *truly* imaginative never otherwise than analytic."[1]

Everything must be questioned, and with unrestrained imagination rather than reason or experience—indeed, "the ingenious are always fanciful."[2] Sometimes the nature of a crime is a simple calculation: the angle of entry and exit wounds can be matched to the angle of attack, the shape and size of the wounds to the caliber of bullet, the caliber of bullet to the gun itself, the gun to its owner, the owner to his motive. Other times it is simple prediction. Today, sophisticated computer models can use publicly available data to pinpoint exactly when and where a crime is likely to occur. In either instance, the crime can nearly always be explained, so long as the calculation adds up or the prediction proves true.

And yet sometimes the nature of the crime cannot be explained. Sometimes there is a body but no murder weapon, no escape route, no plausible motive. Sometimes there are murders most extraordinary, and such murders call for equally extraordinary investigations.

This is where a knowledge of the occult, or that which is "hidden,"[3] can be useful, as its methods of investigation can help tap into a reasoning beyond the known. In other words, the investigation can include what may be referred to by laymen as "supernatural" or "magical" evidence, for lack of better terms.

Similar to evidence that is retrieved via more conventional methods of investigation, all ideas rooted in the supernatural are *essentially real*. In actuality, they are far older than any scientific system currently in favor. As Jung writes in his essay "The Structure and Dynamics of the Psyche:" "Science is simply a matter of intellect, and that the intellect is only one among several fundamental psychic functions and therefore does not suffice to give a complete picture of the world."[4]

Therefore, when what is questioned is beyond the realm of human knowledge, it must rely on psychic functions other than the

1. Edgar Allan Poe, *The Pit and the Pendulum*, Penguin Books, 2009, p. 70.
2. Poe, *The Pit and the Pendulum*, p. 70.
3. See also C.G. Jung's "psychic shadow side," which refers to the unconscious aspect of the personality. As a parallel, the blanket term "occult" is used throughout this introduction to refer to that which is unseen, unsaid, and unheard.
4. C. G. Jung, *Psychology and the Occult*, Princeton University Press, 1977, p. 125.

intellect, namely intuition and speculation. Here, the investigator seeks to create a state of nonbeing, to lose him or herself in the very reality of the criminal. And in doing so, they become a portal from one world to the next—a medium between the physical and spiritual worlds, but always drawing on real-life experience—allowing for explanations previously beyond conception. In this way, the occult investigator may interrogate not just the practical questions of *how* or *when*, but the deeper inquiry of *what* and *why*.

The body in the sound-proof room: A case study

As Jung writes in his essay "The Psychological Foundations of Belief in Spirits": "The 'haunted house' has not yet become extinct even in the most enlightened and the most intellectual cities, nor has the peasant ceased to believe in the bewitching of his cattle. On the contrary, in this age of materialism—the inevitable consequence of rationalistic enlightenment—there has been a revival of the belief in spirits, but this time on a higher level. It is not a relapse into the darkness of superstition, but an intense scientific interest, a need to direct the searchlight of truth on to the chaos of dubious facts."[5]

In the spirit of this "searchlight of truth," let's consider the famous case of the body in the sound-proof room, as recorded in the correspondence of M. Dupré, colleague of world-renowned occult investigator Clouzot.

One dreary autumn day, Dupré and Clouzot were summoned to a manor in the French countryside, where the owner, a famous diplomat and museum benefactor named Bernard, had been discovered murdered.

It's important to mention that this event occurred in the years following World War II, during which Clouzot was deployed to Germany after the Battle of France. And while it's widely believed Clouzot was incarcerated in Stalag IX B for a number of years (as evidenced by Dupré's letters), this has never been confirmed, and Clouzot never spoke of it.

Bernard's manor was provincial in style, with steeply pitched roofs, dormer windows, a stone-lined exterior, and symmetrical

---

5. Jung, *Psychology and the Occult*, p. 109.

chimneys. Despite the hardships suffered by France during the War, Bernard's estate had made it through with the bulk of its grandeur remarkably undiminished. Its grounds were well kept, tended to by nearly twenty servants, with eight staff bedrooms in the main house and two more in the stable house.

Upon arrival, Clouzot walked the raked gravel walkways, all of which converged upon the house, his hands tucked into the pockets of his gray raincoat. He inspected the latches on the windows and checked for boot prints in the soil beds. He wandered the hedgerows and spent time communing with the horses in the stalls. When he was satisfied he had a lay of the land, he went inside.

There, a grand foyer led to a beautiful, wrapping staircase. The fixtures were gold, the wallpaper imported from faraway lands, and the art antiquarian. One prominent painting depicted an ancient stone arch that looked decidedly Greek. Another depicted the Roman Forum. And yet another depicted an early Gothic castle nestled among emerald trees.

Clouzot's footsteps echoed through the large rooms as he moved about the house. He inspected a number of maps, papers, and correspondence in Bernard's study as well as the books in the two-story library. Of note were several titles by renowned occultists, mystics, and theologians, including Ernst Schertel, Meister Eckhart, Nicolas Flamel, and the Count of St. Germain. He also spent quite some time studying a ledger in the wood-paneled office, its pages filled with long sequences of numbers.

"What's that there?" Dupré asked, lighting his tobacco pipe.

"A farmer's almanac," Clouzot said.

"The manor has a working farm," said the stone-faced butler, hovering near the doorway.

"That it does." Clouzot closed the almanac and turned to the butler. "I'm ready to see the body."

Dupré and Clouzot were escorted upstairs to one of the manor's numerous bedrooms. There, the butler turned a sconce on the wall, which opened a secret panel and revealed a room within the room. The walls and ceiling of this smaller room were lined with thick, heavy foam sheets, effectively rendering it sound proof. A padded restraint chair with a peculiarly high, ornate headrest had been bolted to the floor, its various straps still buckled. Behind the chair stood an electric lamp.

It was dark and difficult to see. However, lantern light revealed the body of Bernard—if one can refer to it as such—spread all over the room. Viscera dripped slowly from the ceiling. Skull fragments, brain matter, and shattered bones and teeth were scattered across the floor. And there, in the seat of the chair, a single large clump of clotted blood, hair, muscle, and bone sat quivering as if pressed in a terrine. A fully intact eyeball stared outward unblinking from within this gelatinous form, forever fixated on Bernard's final, agonizing moments.

As the butler explained, his voice unsteady with emotion, Bernard had taken his supper at the regular hour the night before. Then he drank a single glass of cognac and smoked a cigar in his study, where he reviewed his ledger for quite some time. Afterward, he requested to be strapped into the chair.

"The door can only be opened from the outside," the butler explained. "I was instructed to turn on the electric lamp, seal the chamber, and return only at sunrise. This—" he gestured at the mound of flesh and bone on the chair "—was what I found. You cannot imagine my horror."

Carefully avoiding the puddled gore and clumps of hair and teeth, Clouzot tried a few of the straps on the chair, which held fast. He turned on the electric lamp, walked a circle around the chair, then turned it off. "Was this a regular habit of your master?"

"Every so often. Perhaps twice a year."

Clouzot seemed to consider this. "How long had Bernard lived in this house?"

"Since he was a child, monsieur."

"He never lived anywhere else?"

"No, monsieur."

"Thank you," Clouzot told the butler. "You may take your leave."

Surprised, the butler looked to Dupré, who, long accustomed to his friend's eccentricities, merely smiled and shrugged.

The butler exhaled loudly, bowed his head, and left the room.

"Quite the mess," said Dupré, puffing on his pipe. "What do you make of it?"

Clouzot slowly shook his head. "I can't say for sure. At least not yet." He knelt to take a closer look at the viscera on the floor. Then once again he turned on the electric lamp, noting how the chair's high headrest cast an intricate shadow on the floor.

Suddenly, the look on his face changed, as if "overcome by profound realization," writes Dupré. "I had seen this look come over my old friend's face on numerous occasions, and always I took it to mean his mind's eye had focused on some ghastly sight hidden from us mere mortals."[6]

"You're not going to like this, old friend," Clouzot said. "But to fully understand what's happened to Bernard, we're going to need to clean up this mess. Then I'm going to need you to strap me into this chair."

Knowing how fruitless it would be to argue with his famous friend, Dupré did as was requested. Together, they collected the largest fragments of Bernard they could find and gave the room a deep scrubbing. The fragments, Clouzot explained, would be sent away for testing overnight.

Dupré then installed Clouzot securely into the seat's restraints and clicked on the lamp. He saw how the light cast shadows across the floor, and how Clouzot, with his head strapped in place, could not look away from these shadows. Then he sealed his friend away under instruction to not return until the next morning.

"Under no circumstances," Clouzot had said, "must I be interrupted. Promise me."

"You have my word."

Come morning, an anxious Dupré, accompanied by the incredulous butler, opened the sound-proof room and, with utmost relief, freed Clouzot from the contraption.

Noticeably the worse for wear, Clouzot said, "Gentlemen, the mystery is solved." He adjusted his collar and tie. He was weak in Dupré's arms. "But first, a cup of hot coffee with ample sugar and cream is in order. I'm afraid I didn't sleep a wink."

Reality checking: The impossible is not only plausible but also possible

A crime is anything that goes against the natural order of things

6. Matthieu Dupré, *The Collected Correspondence*, Volume I, Brown University Press, 1985, p. 203.

and inflicts harm on an individual in the material world. Here, the natural order of things typically refers to civil laws and historical precedent. In regard to the occult, however, it can also refer to the laws of both physics and metaphysics.

Any event—any crime, for that matter—is part of its inheritable past. For example, the gelatinous form found in the soundproof room was once the man known as Bernard. This is an objective truth. The iris in the intact eyeball matched his eye color (green flecked with brown). In addition, the teeth recovered matched Bernard's dental records, samples matched his blood type (B-negative, exceedingly rare), and the print taken from an intact finger also produced a match.

In this way occult investigations must take into account two types of evidence. On the one hand, there are the standard facts proven by reality, and on the other hand, there are the facts with no inheritable past. Such evidence must therefore be selected and evaluated in a manner that displaces the fact beyond observation.

The occult method of investigation changes the way we consider not only the *plausibility* of the crime but also its very *possibility*. It is a matter of not simply asking questions and expecting to arrive at an answer, but rather allowing possible answers to inform the asking of questions. This is the difference between "what has occurred" and "what has occurred that has never occurred before," as differentiated in Poe's "Murders in the Rue Morgue."

According to the "ontological principle" posited by Alfred North Whitehead, the philosopher perhaps most concerned with the complexities of reality, "Actual entities are the only *reasons*; so that to search for a *reason* is to search for one or more actual entities."[7]

For Whitehead, "actual entities" are the foundational elements of reality. They are either temporal (occasions of experience) or atemporal (God, or the principle of concretion that advances all things toward more complex forms).

Removed from any theological implication, this distinction is useful in that it illustrates how the material world can be "overlaid" with a lattice of truths beyond our grasp. Things are always

7. Alfred North Whitehead, *Process and Reality*, the Free Press, New York, 1978, p. 24.

moving from one state of possibility to another. And if we are attuned to the right frequencies, perhaps, we may sense the gap between these two states—the passage of time and space that opens between one state and another, something we may slip into —and come to understand how it informs the nature of the crime.

This process is known as "reality checking," in which concepts of what is real in our waking state are "checked" against what is real in our unconscious states, therefore helping the investigator reach conclusions beyond logic.

All of this, of course, is covered in much more depth in this textbook (in particular, the 62 categories of satisfactory explanation, as well as Sections III and IV). For now, we seek only to highlight how the occult element changes the line of questioning. In other words, "What if the so-called natural order of things did not adhere to any underlying laws of nature?"

Considering how the occult detective's role as medium between the physical and spiritual worlds draws on real-life experience, it can be quite dangerous to escape whatever liminal state is entered. Some people lose themselves in the deep folds of memory. Others become untethered from reality and are doomed to wander shadow realms for eternity.

Therefore, reality checking requires an immense amount of caution on the part of the investigator and should not be entered into without the proper conditioning.

The body in the sound-proof room: A case study (concluded)

Now then, we return to the words of Poe: "To look at a star by glance—to view it in a side-long way, by turning toward it the exterior portions of the *retina* (more susceptible of feeble impressions of light than the interior), is to behold the star distinctly—is to have the best appreciation of its lustre—a lustre which grows dim just in proportion as we turn our vision *fully* upon it."[8]

Thus, things that blind (the spectacle) must be considered from new angles, and the investigator must consider how appearance hides the true nature of an object (the occult).

Clouzot sat at the head of the long table in the dining room,

---

8. Poe, *The Pit and the Pendulum*, pp. 82–83.

patiently stirring his coffee. The full staff of the manor—servants, cooks, cleaners, farmers, groundskeeper, and stable hands—stood along the paneled walls, hands clasped in anticipation. Finally, Clouzot raised the cup to his lips, took a long, satisfied sip, and began his explanation.

"Upon arrival, I immediately noticed the house was built at the epicenter of clearly marked gravel walkways that cut through the grounds. Based on the late Bernard's particular interests, I soon surmised these walkways corresponded with several well-known local ley lines. Ley lines, of course, are alignments between sites of energetic significance. I envisioned these lines as if from the point of view of a passing raven, and soon matched this pattern to a number of diagrams found throughout the house, including the design carved into the headrest of the chair in the hidden room, thus confirming my theory. Seven lines, forming seven angles, each of which carry its own energy. It seems our man Bernard had quite the fixation on this design.

"From there, several antiquarian paintings took my attention. For instance, the painting of the ancient stone arch depicts the Cape Matapan Caves along the coast of the Ionian Sea. The Roman Forum is noteworthy because of the nearby Lacus Curtius pit. And the Gothic castle depicted is none other than Houska Castle found in the countryside of Prague, all-too-recently occupied by the Nazis. What do these have in common? Well, each depicts an ancient archeological site at one point considered to be the mouth of Hell."

The butler and several servants gasped. "He lies," someone murmured.

Clouzot continued unperturbed. "Many of the books in the library betray a keen interest in meditation, astral projection, and spiritualism. Most notable, however, are the books by Ernst Schertel, the man whose book on magic is said to have been carefully studied by Hitler himself."

More gasps. A few of the younger women left the room.

"I'll admit I was initially unsure what to make of the sequences of numbers written in the ledger." He smiled knowingly at Dupré. "But after checking the values against the farmer's almanac, I realized they quantified weather patterns related to certain atmospheric pressures."

Clouzot addressed the butler. "How often did you say Bernard requested to be strapped into the chair?"

"Twice per year, monsieur."

"No doubt on those days when the alignment of pressures was strongest along the ley lines. When the atmosphere itself was literally charged with electricity, that strangest and most untamable of physical phenomena."

Clouzot paused and took another sip of his coffee.

"Ladies and gentlemen, I can see from your faces that you are not following. Perhaps it would be helpful if I explained what happened to me once I was strapped into the chair and sealed away in the sound-proof room.

"My gaze was fixed on the shadows cast across the floor in the otherwise dark room. At first, my breathing slowed. My ears no longer picked up any external noise. I became aware of the pulse of blood in my veins. Every sound from within my own body was amplified. I wiggled my fingers and heard the grinding of my bones. I heard every thundering beat of my heart, every swish of blood as it coursed through my veins.

"There is no telling how much time passed. Eons, perhaps. Eventually, I focused on the spaces between the shadowy lines, and envisioned myself surrounded by a solid wall of red. As this wall closed around me, I saw tiny spaces emerge, small black holes arranged in a perfect pattern. The closer I got to pure color, the more I saw it as a delicate balance of colors previously unseen.

"It occurred to me, strapped there in that chair, that when we dream we wake into new worlds. And so I began to dream. I dreamed of houses within houses, rooms overlapping other rooms, and the intersection of new and dizzying dimensions in between.

"Think, ladies and gentlemen, of seven angles, seven corners, in seven different houses in seven different dimensions, all of which share a single focal point—a room within a room designed to channel their energies. Indeed, the shadows cast by the head rest of the chair aligned perfectly with this nexus—a focal point designed to channel the power of the person strapped into the chair. Now, imagine the ears inside this person opening to sounds previously unheard, and entering a portal between worlds.

"I felt the energies from these seven dimensions all flow into and through one another, unspooling a web of such brilliant design, with me at its center. And in this state, and with the right electrical charges in the atmosphere, came to understand how a person's spirit might theoretically leave his body and transcend to a higher plane of reality.

"Imagine the horror I felt as my spirit began to climb out of my body, as if a prisoner fleeing his prison, desperate to join a realm more to its liking. I knew that if my spirit succeeded in this task, it would take my very strength with it, leaving only my body to succumb to impossible forces.

"And so I brought myself to the very brink of this realization only to ground myself in reality, thinking only of what was real, allowing myself only to believe in what was possible. I recalled simple sensations." He smelled his coffee and took a sip. "The smell of coffee. The way wind ripples the surface of still ponds. The feeling of rose petals between two fingers. And in this way, I endured the seemingly endless passage of time until my friend here returned to free me from the chair."

Clouzot finished the rest of his coffee, and Dupré noticed how his old friend's "hand shook, almost imperceptibly, as if rocked by the implications of his own words. It was the kind of thing that only an old friend would notice. Something that, in turn, shook me to my core. Only imagine the torture poor Clouzot must have endured in those long hours, strapped to that chair in that darkened cell, an all-too-terrifying echo of his time in the German work camps. Surely, the roar of the world's silence was overwhelming. I shudder to think of what he must have overcome, even to this day."[9]

"It's outrageous," the butler said.

Clouzot leveled his gaze at the butler. "More outrageous than finding the eviscerated remains of your master after he was locked away in a room with no exit?"

The butler's face flushed and he lowered his eyes.

"Now then," Clouzot continued. "Every crime surely has its motive, and this one is no exception. Let us once more return to the facts at hand."

He reached into his breast pocket and placed a neatly folded letter on the table.

---

9. Dupré, *The Collected Correspondence*, Vol. I, p. 204.

"As evidenced by the collection of books in Bernard's library," Clouzot said, speaking slowly, "it's clear he believed he could transcend his physical form and use his body as a key to gateways beyond." He tapped the letter with two fingers. "This letter confirms that Bernard's experiments with interdimensional transference were part of a larger, more sinister plan."

He turned to the butler. "You said that Bernard lived in this house his entire life, yes?"

The butler nodded. "Yes."

"Which means he never enlisted in the army," Clouzot said. "Nor did he flee the country during the occupation."

"That's enough," the butler shouted. "You offend us with these damnable fantasies."

"Fantasies? Come now. Then how else to explain this letter I found among Bernard's correspondence? Feel free to peruse it yourselves. It details the ongoing efforts shared by the master of this house and the Nazis toward the end of the war. You'll see the signature and stamp at the bottom belong to none other than Heinrich Himmler."

More gasps.

"But what does it all mean?" Dupré said.

"I'm glad you asked, old friend. It means that the childhood home of Bernard just so happens to have been built on a site of great spiritual significance. Knowing this, the Nazis likely spared his life during the occupation in exchange for his help and knowledge regarding the occult. In return, we can only assume he was offered great power. After the war ended and Hitler was presumed dead, Bernard turned his attention to opening a doorway to Hell, from which he planned to free the imprisoned spirit of Hitler himself and thus fulfill his destiny. Luckily for us, he succeeded only in internalizing destructive forces beyond his control. He forgot the simple truth that reality as we know it, despite its frequent horrors, remains safe in its very knowability. As far out as we travel, we must always return home. Bernard channeled seven realities all at once, each of which exerted different laws of nature, and when he opened his mind to this reality, when he let go of those things tethering him to the earth, he was ripped apart and crushed and exploded all at the same time."

And with that, the case of the body in the sound-proof room was closed.

In closing: Questioning the way things are

As Dupin says in Poe's "The Purloined Letter," "The principle of the *vis inertiæ*... seems to be identical in physics and metaphysics. It is not more true in the former, that a large body is with more difficulty set in motion than a smaller one, and that its subsequent *momentum* is commensurate with this difficulty, than it is, in the latter, that intellects of the vaster capacity, while more forcible, more constant, and more eventful in their movements than those of the inferior grade, are yet the less readily moved, and more embarrassed and full of hesitation in the first few steps of their progress."[10]

The investigator must always question *the way things are*, and the more he or she believes things are the way they are because "that's how it's always been," the less effective he or she will be as an investigator.

To be truly effective, you must follow your intuition. As Jung writes, "The effect of intuition on man is indeed very similar to the instant fascination which smells have for animals."[11] And in this way, man can intuit just as a dog would smell bloodstains hidden beneath a carpet.

So, what does this textbook offer you? Perhaps it offers guidance around how to see what isn't there—and what that means for your methods of investigation. Perhaps it serves as a playbook for how to conduct an investigation. Or perhaps it provides only so much nonsense. This depends entirely on how you choose to receive its messages.

However they are received, it is our hope that the following text explores the concepts of occult methods of investigation with scientific rigor and provides case studies that can guide you in your career. It also offers conflict resolution strategies to deal with colleagues who will, inevitably, disagree with your beliefs, methods, and opinions. And in this way, it will likely prove most useful, as

---

10. Poe, *The Pit and the Pendulum*, p. 117.
11. Jung, *Psychology and the Occult*, p. 152.

you will no doubt encounter your fair share of skepticism—if not outright hostility—when drawing your conclusions.

—For Gordon B. White

The God of Rust

Jocelyn Szczepaniak-Gillece

THE SUMMER HAD BEEN UNUSUALLY hot, though "unusually hot" was such a common term that it had become meaningless. Still, the summer before had been a little cooler which meant this summer was functionally hotter. Everything was unusual so nothing really was anymore.

But the heat had affected the garden in ways that were increasingly difficult to ignore. Where the tart cherry tree had once borne fruit in such great quantities that its limbs brushed gracefully against its trunk like a dancer's sweeping bow, now the young couple was lucky to get a handful. And what can you do with a handful of cherries; hardly enough for jam, just enough to mock your desire to preserve some of summer's red.

Tomatoes swelled but didn't ripen. The onions sent up green shoots but shrank underground into pale and flaccid bulbs. Potato blossoms turned sky blue and round like coloring book flowers, but the roots curled up and dented at the slightest touch. There were herbs, still, but one can't live on rosemary. One can only crush it between thumb and forefinger, sniff, and remember what it was like to live with bounty and hope in more usual times.

The food losses could be amended by carefully budgeted trips to the market, Sarah assured herself. But fear that this harvest wasn't the only bad one crackled toward the back of her scalp.

That this was merely a symptom of something much bigger than her garden.

She said goodbye to her husband as he departed for another autumn and half a winter away on contracting business, maintaining plumbing systems in a desolate land decimated by invasions and warfare. Or was he advising local leaders on how to maintain voting practices in an unstable country? Whatever it was this time, and she knew better than to ask specifics, Joshua was off again on assignment and she had only to feed herself for a few months with whatever made it back in wire transfers.

They would still be able to talk while he was gone, at least now and then. His corporation sponsored members and their spouses for the newest implant tech so that no call would be missed for lack of a charge or a lost device. Sarah touched hers absently, rubbing her index finger on the smooth healed-over bump to the side of her tragus as though it would make him contact her sooner.

The vegetables were terrible in their own way, but the most depressing part of the garden trouble was the rust on the elderberry bush. She didn't even need the elderberries; mostly she let the birds, what was left of them, pick at the purple flesh, then felt less guilty for not spending on seed. But the leaves were so lacy and sweet, the canes so tall and slender, the flowers so fragrant, the bush hardly a bush at all, more like a canopy from a Japanese brush painting, such that she could imagine herself laying underneath it wrapped in silk chirimen next to a shamisen player as lazy afternoons turned slowly to night.

Now, though, the fronded green fingers contorted into orange and brown claws, measly and defective. She'd never seen a brush painting that showed a tree infected with mold. No one wanted to stare at something suffering the consequences of unusual heat and the consequent awakening of ancient pestilence. When her elderberry withered, the garden turned from an idyll of imagination and transcendent art into a microcosm of worldly toil where the realities of existence came crashing into her headspace and demanded to be heard.

Her painting tore. Her tree shrank back into a shrub. Her garden turned to an image of the wider world and its wreckage.

It was, she thought, all of a piece, how unusually hot it had been, how her garden that had once been so lush had turned over to rot, how the money had slowly started to dry up even as her husband was gone for longer and longer spells, how she couldn't seem to keep a baby inside of her past the two-month mark.

Nothing would grow right, nothing in the garden, nothing in the bank accounts, nothing in her body. It was a curse, but whether it was hers to bear or one she merely shared in was impossible for her to parse.

~

THE ELDERBERRY TOOK on a bilious cast that made the whole plant look feeble. But even as the leaves succumbed to infection they refused to fall, instead hanging there in a mockery of health and beauty. Sarah stared at it from the window, wanting to tear the fronds from the branches but unable to bring herself to risk harm to the tree.

She tried not to give in to despair and mostly failed. She tried to mark the weeks her husband had been gone by how many leaves rotted. Three weeks, about. She looked onto her garden and wished for growth.

She spoke to her husband when he could call her, which was only every few days. It was busy, he said, and dangerous. The country was even more desiccated than he remembered; there were more impenetrably hot days and fewer cool nights. The sparse clinics were overrun by rampant infection from contaminated water. The people were more desperate than ever, and in them he saw something of his own future. Though his voice vibrated directly into her cochlea from the tiny metal implant, he sounded tinny and so, so distant.

Autumn turned. The loneliness became its own kind of companion.

~

A MONTH after Joshua left Sarah was due to bleed again, but she didn't.

At first she thought it couldn't really be possible, could it, he'd been gone this whole time. But it made a certain kind of sense, what with all the burdens of late, that this one would arrive at the same time.

Of course she'd be pregnant when he wasn't coming home for another five months. Of course she'd have to suffer alone through several weeks of morning sickness followed by hours of solitary pain as her warped body shunted out something sickly and unformed.

It was a cruel joke her brain played on her, the tempering of frustration and injury with something akin to hope. But there it was anyway, like a firefly blinking on in the corner of her eye at sunset, even though the fireflies were long extinct.

Sarah stood under the elderberry and held one of its rusted leaves, marveling at how the orange dust coated her palms. She wiped her hands across her torso where her shirt met her waist-band. A muddy brown sparrow landed a foot or so away and dug for leftover berries.

Such an awful bird, she thought, invasive little shit. She watched it idly as it hopped from branch to branch, pecking at any cluster it could find.

But within a few minutes Sarah's curiosity turned to slow dawning disgust: where the sparrow's feathers drifted along the leaves, the rust clung to them, such that what was once dun-colored was now an angry orange. Its beady brown eye rolled in an orange socket, and its beak was coated in glaring color. It stared at her, irradiated, looking like a harbinger of decay and a messenger of unnatural apocalypse.

Sarah looked down at her waist, stunned to see the same on herself: streaks of thick orange crisscrossing her belly not only where her hands had gone but also where other branches had brushed by in the gently moving air. She, too, was covered in rust, and as she lifted her shirt she saw it was not only her clothes but her stomach painted in garish bright stripes directly over where the baby, anemic as it might be, was growing.

She took three showers but her torso still glowed in tiger pelt patterns. It pulsed at night with a steady, dull heat.

～

THE WEEKS WENT by without incident, which was incident in itself. When she made it to three weeks past the positive test, she marveled at how far she'd come; half her earlier pregnancies had been inelegantly complete by this point, the other half by two months in. As much as she scrubbed, faint orange was still visible across her stomach. In some ways, she was beginning to appreciate how the lines flowed like brushstrokes over her growing bump.

Her implant throbbed every few days with a brief call from Joshua. His group had met with some trouble at a border between territories; thank God there had been military security present to back his team up. The gunfire had been upsetting, but he'd managed to hide in the truck until the shooting stopped and didn't let his eyes stray from the road ahead until he was long past. It was sensorily confusing, how his voice was both beamed directly into her head and from a very far distance, how he was entirely present within her and as removed physically from her as he could be.

That wasn't so far from how she was starting to think about her own body, which both housed her organs and incubated a strange alien being. The baby wasn't an alien, that wasn't the right word choice for a nervously optimistic soon-to-be-mother, but it was completely unfamiliar and she just didn't really know what exactly would come out.

If it came out in one piece.

It was that very fear that kept her from telling Joshua just yet. That and the tension in the desert, how it seemed like a switch might get flipped at any moment and explosions would ring in the air, golden and glowing and cascading like arched fireworks until they hit the ground.

Although the rest of the trees outside also looked like fireworks with their branches lit up in flaming shades, the elderberry still hadn't loosed its leaves. They too were bright; if anything, the rust had gotten even brighter, decorating them with a fierceness the color of battle.

Now in the middle part of autumn when the wonders of nature were found in the dying off, Sarah was starting to think it beautiful. She let her fingers graze the leaves, no longer afraid of the rust coming off on her nails; after all, she couldn't ever get it fully off, so what was the worry?

It didn't sicken her. In fact, could it be that she felt stronger than ever, even with the fetus sucking out her energy? And it did seem to be drawing significantly from her; she was gaining weight quickly in the middle, her belly protruding much further than it should be just at the start of the second trimester, and she was hungry all the time.

But the garden was taking care of her. Inexplicably, it had started producing. Although the tomato plants were long done for the year, something told her to leave the yellowed stems up. And now, halfway through November, they were laden with rich, nearly bursting red fruit.

The zucchini bushes sloughed off their powdery mildew and sent out an abundance of vigorous new crop. When she dug up the last of the potatoes, she found to her astonishment that they had twined their roots underneath the perennials; full and luscious Dutch yellows clustered among the asters and the lavender and came popping out of the ground like eyes from children's toys. They were so creamy and tender that all she needed to savor them was a pinch of sea salt.

Sarah barely needed to shop, but one evening ran out of butter. The line to get into the market was long; there was word of shortages from a bad season and from all the wars breaking out abroad. Once she finally made it through the doors, she was forced to buy margarine because the cows had stopped producing since the last time she'd bought dairy.

When she returned home hours later, it was dark. She hadn't left a light on, and when she toddled awkwardly and unbalanced up the path she found her breath catching in her throat. What if she tripped? What if she fell belly-first and hurt the baby? She felt tears rise in her eyes at the thought and stumbled, panicked.

And then the elderberry blinked on. Its leaves glowed warmly, cozy and artificial like a gas fireplace. Some of the rust blew off in the breeze and landed on the pathway, lighting the way forward and to her door.

When she walked by the tree it seemed to bow gently toward her. Unconsciously, she bowed back. Once she found her way inside she wolfed down two huge tomatoes. The juices ran down her chin and stained her shirt like rivulets of blood.

∼

AFTER THAT NIGHT, Sarah didn't really need to go to the store anymore. She lost her taste for dairy and there wasn't any available except on the black market, and she knew so few people in town nor could she afford the prices. Not just dairy; anything but vegetables turned her stomach.

There was no reason for worry because Sarah ate often and well. She spent most of her time eating or thinking about what she would want to eat next. And there was no reason to worry about that either because Sarah had so many choices. Vegetables and fruits sprang up like ragweed, tall and life-giving and delicious, tasting of pure nutrient and sunny pleasure. Even things she didn't remember planting, like ground-cherries and nasturtium with their edible peppery blossoms and strawberries and delicata squash, all of it, everywhere, spinach and bitter greens and peas threading between the larger plants.

Maybe seeds from a cast away core, or spat months ago from between her teeth?

If she thought too much about it, it didn't make any sense; blackberry bushes, unbidden? Pumpkins, ripening alongside cucumbers? Everything fitting perfectly as it could, no need to prune or amend or water?

But why think about it with anything but gratitude, she decided. After all, Joshua's calls told her only about starvation and turmoil, death and despair. Why worry when the soil was giving? When she was nestled in luxury like a child of Eden?

Little molecules of rust drifted lazily around the garden and settled on everything growing. She found it in the mornings on her pillow in the shape of her head, and it made her feel like she was painted by Titian, her body swelling in seductive waves, her hair strung with metallic pigments. She was a flame-haired angel, a being of spirit and body, and she tore leaves from the elderberry and festooned her massive belly with their gleaming natural paints until she shone like a bride ornamented for marriage to some ancient god.

When Joshua called, she barely spoke. She let him talk and then rubbed her temple to end the call. Because what could she say to him that he would understand? And by now, there wasn't much she took from him for comfort.

Her body was enormous and held all that she needed: the baby growing and pulsing inside her, her insides strengthened by fibrous filaments, her blood fed by the rust that feathered all the crops with something that looked like iron oxide. She had become a body sustained by what she had, the garden and its bounty, the knowledge that she was both entirely of this parcel of land and of something bigger, and the new creatures that she soon would see, both the one inside of her and the one she was in the process of becoming.

And so she soon wanted nothing of anything else, nothing at all but what there was. Though the weather had turned and the cold winds blew, in her garden it was eternal late summer. She walked naked through it, her belly distended and heavy, her skin streaked with coppery rust, plucking fruits from trees and lying under the sun, letting the vegetation stroke her body like a team of chambermaids readying her for the sacraments she would soon endure.

She slept outside, too, and the elderberry leaves whispered stories in her ears to ease her way, and she dreamt of stems and stalks and seeds and breezes colored orange that blew what once she thought was disease in susurrating swarms that suffocated the entire world.

THE IMPLANT OFFENDED HER, and so she plucked it out with a branch from the elderberry sharpened on a stone. If it hurt, she soon forgot, because the gaping wound was quickly plugged with a coat of orange rust left by the branch. It mingled with the blood running down her face and neck such that all she wore was this ferrous coating like a wild-eyed acolyte of a secret sect.

The only things she thought of were the baby and its father. He was, she now knew without knowing, not Joshua after all. He was something magnificent who had sent very long fingers out to touch her, who had sent his seed to find its way inside her and ready her for his coming and the new world that followed. She had been chosen by the god of pestilence, and she awaited his arrival.

If it was fair or not didn't matter to her. What was fair anymore, anyway? If rot is what we're all meant for, why not be its bride? Why not reign alongside it in glory when it comes to claim its throne?

All day and all night she lay under the elderberry in a fiery haze. Everything appeared to her behind an orange screen, like her eyes had turned to heat sensors. Her body was wracked with throbbing pain.

The baby and its father were on their way.

~

JOSHUA'S CONTRACT had run out. Though it took nearly two weeks, it was a miracle he made it back home at all; so few airplanes were cleared to leave and so many ports closed. The seas roiled with unpredictable force and even the biggest boats risked capsizing. There was little fuel and Joshua paid whatever drivers he could find with the last of his cash, which, he was sure, was well on its way to being useless. Whatever lay on the horizon was far from appealing, no matter what part of the world he might be in.

But Sarah, he thought, Sarah was at home. Even if he hadn't been able to talk to her in two months, Sarah must be there. And so he traveled long and hard roads to be with the wife at the end of the world.

When he arrived at last, depleted in mind and body, he was somehow unsurprised at much of what greeted him: a house ill-maintained, overgrown vines choking the downspouts and black mold speckling the siding. Thick and gnarled stems twisted up around the porch and the front door, snarling any attempt to ring the bell or turn the knob.

Joshua dropped his torn bag and went to the garden, searching for a second way in.

Their little plot of land, once so carefully kept, was a thicket of thorns and branches. He took out a pocket knife and hacked through what he could until the growth gave way. A thin tunnel opened up, just about the size of a man. He followed it through darkness toward a pulsing orange glow.

There he found his wife, naked and soaked in blood, supine under the elderberry tree. Every bit of her, even the whites of her eyes, was coated in rust like she was a prehistoric iron figure unearthed from the damp. Her mouth lay slack and her belly heaved and fell with the effects of struggle. Nestled between her wet legs lay the source of that struggle.

At first it looked like a massive carnelian, glittering and faceted, but as he stared the image clarified. Underneath the coating of Sarah's internal gore, which gave it a gemlike glimmer, was a seedpod the size of a child covered all over in orange rust. It glowed from the inside, silhouetting something red and sharp and furious that spasmed and shrieked and beat at the walls that held it. The seam that ran all the way around shuddered and strained along with Sarah's ragged breath.

Up above, the thicket drew back to reveal a sky no longer heavy with ice storms but with the weight of a massive orange sun. Sweat streamed from every pore on Joshua's body as the rays shattered atmospheric protections and sent radiation surging down from the sky. The wet ground sizzled and turned the vegetation instantly toward decay and an overpowering smell of rot filled his nostrils and throat.

Intense and brutal heat forced Joshua to his knees. The pod shook and began to rip itself apart at the seams. Unlike those who came before, what came from it would know how best to thrive in a cruel new world.

We Didn't Used to Be Like This

Jack Klausner

THE THOUGHT SURFACES UNBIDDEN, like a submerged corpse heaving up from black water, bloated, bobbing. I'm sitting with my wife and my daughter on our patio at the rear of the house, in the sunshine, butterflies and bees hovering audibly over the wildflower borders. Suddenly, everything seems restless and fidgety in the warm breeze.

Is everything all right, Derek? Lianne asks.

Yeah, Dad, says Rhiannon, looking up from her mobile. You've got a weird look on your face.

Lianne sips of white wine from her glass, then reaches over and puts a hand on top of mine.

Derek? she says.

We didn't used to be like this.

I'm fine, I tell her. I'm fine.

~

RHIANNON FINDS THE FIRST PHOTOGRAPH. She likes to rearrange her bedroom every few months, shifting the bed to a different wall or pushing the chest of drawers or her writing desk to a different position. I asked about it once. She said she liked the change, the new configurations. A new way of being, she said, until she felt the need to change it all again.

She was moving her wardrobe—walking it in a rocking motion from one side of the bedroom to the other—when she discovered the photograph: a girl's tiny face staring up from the carpet. Rhiannon shows it to us at the dinner table that night. Like a mugshot, is how she describes it. On inspecting the photograph, Lianne and I are inclined to agree.

Isn't that the daughter of the people who used to live here? Lianne asks.

I thought that girl was younger, Rhiannon says.

I don't know, I reply.

She looks like a serial killer, Rhiannon says. She's holding the photograph up in front of her face.

Don't be cruel, Lianne says. No one looks good in passport photos.

~

LATER, in bed, in the dark, Lianne drapes an arm across my chest.

You've been quiet all evening, she says.

I open my mouth to respond, but am struck by a feeling of déjà vu. Lying in bed, in the dark. My wife resting her arm on my chest and asking me a question—although it isn't a question this time around.

What was *last* time around?

I'm fine, I tell her.

You don't seem fine, Lianne whispers, her lips brushing against my ear. She runs a hand down my chest, over my stomach. Her fingertips find the waistband of my boxer shorts. She bites my earlobe.

~

I FIND THE SECOND PHOTOGRAPH. Lianne is at work and Rhiannon is at school, but I have the day off. I'm in the second reception room and the sunlight is coming in through the venetians, bathing the parquet floor in a warm glow. We use the room as an office-come-library. Bookshelves line the walls, and there's an armchair covered in throws in one corner, near the window. This is where I'm sitting, reading Nabokov's *Despair*, when it catches my eye: a jagged bit of white, peeking over the edge of one of one of the shelves on the opposite wall, in the spot where I had taken the book from the shelf.

What I discover is another passport photograph. A man, this time. Middle-aged, washed-out face looking straight at the camera. White background.

I stand in the sunlight, the wooden floor warm beneath my feet. I stand there looking at the photograph. I look for too long, perhaps.

This unmoored feeling, just briefly. But then it's gone.

IN THE NIGHT I wake up and go to the bathroom. I pad along the landing in the dark, the landing which for some reason feels…not unfamiliar, but somehow foreign. Like I shouldn't be there. Like this is someone else's house.

After flushing the toilet I go to the sink and splash my face with cold water. When I look up at the mirror, what's there is a reflection that isn't mine, but that of the man in the photograph.

I blink and the reflection is my own again, waxy and pale from the light above the mirror. Shadows pool in the contours of my face in such a way as to echo a skull.

I splash my face with cold water again.

I TELL Rhiannon about the dream over breakfast the next morning. This is how I have squared the incident with the mirror in my mind: as a dream.

I'm telling her about it when I notice her hair, which is tied up in a messy bun, which I haven't seen her do before. Or have I? I ask her about it.

Felt like a change, she says, her right cheek bulging with toast.

Is that mascara?

A brief pause. Then she says, I've worn makeup to school for ages.

Have you?

Yes.

She shoves the last of the toast into her mouth and gets up and goes out of the kitchen. I listen to the rustle of her picking up her school bag from the hallway floor, then the front door opening. I expect, strangely, to hear traffic, the murmur of a town morning, as though our front door opened straight on to the pavement of a busy street. I don't know why. There is of course only quiet, the faint sound of a lone bird singing, followed by a loud thud as the front door swings heavily shut.

~

SHE'S DIFFERENT, I tell Lianne when she comes downstairs.

She's just growing up, that's all.

A wave of familiarity—I have had this conversation before, here, in the kitchen, and just like now she was leaning against the countertop, me standing in front of her, and it was morning and time to leave soon for the office.

Are you all right, Derek?

Déjà vu, I reply.

Lianne follows me into the hallway, where I put on my shoes. At the front door she kisses me goodbye. As her face gets closer, and as it drifts away again, I am struck by the idea that she, too, is somehow wrong. That there is something incorrect about her, in a way I can't explain.

What? she says.

The other side of the hedge, there is the sound of our neighbour's footsteps on his long gravel driveway as he heads to his car. There is the sound of the car door opening, then closing, followed by the purr of the Jaguar's engine.

Have you done something different today? I ask Lianne.

She frowns. Different in what way?

I don't know.

She looks down for a moment, frowning, thinking. Then she brightens suddenly and looks at me again. I tried a new foundation, she says. What do you think?

It's nice, I reply.

It isn't her foundation. It's not makeup or hair or clothes. It's something else but I don't know what.

I kiss her goodbye again and head to the car.

∾

AT THE OFFICE they tell me I am distracted. At lunchtime, instead of going out with the others I go out to the car and wind the window down and drink San Pelligrino. The sycamore at the edge of the car park sways in the wind, shadow twitching on the ground. I try to picture my wife. I try to identify the thing that seemed wrong about her. Then I think about Rhiannon, how at breakfast it had seemed like her hair, then her makeup, but it wasn't those things, not really. There was something else, less obvious, less tangible. And, I begin to think, something not necessarily new. As though the difference had in fact been there for some time, rendering it oddly familiar despite the strangeness.

I crush the empty water bottle and shove it in the door pocket. As I do so, something catches my eye, and I reach into the door pocket and retrieve the third photograph.

∾

AFTER DINNER I tell Lianne about the photograph I found on the bookshelf. Then I tell her about the photograph in the car.

It must have been carried in on something, she says.

What do you mean?

Into the car, she says. It must have been stuck on something and that's how it got in there.

Lianne is loading the dishwasher. I leave her and go back to the dining table, where the three photographs are arranged. The photograph in the car was a polaroid of a woman, her head and shoulders. She has dark hair and an oval face much like Lianne's. There is a sense that she is startled, as though the photographer crept up on her. Behind her is a green-blue wall, the same colour as the wall in our lounge. When I point this out, Lianne says this is further proof of her theory.

It's the woman who used to live here, she says. One of us has brought it into the car, somehow. It probably got stuck to something.

Don't you think any of this is strange? I ask.

Strange? Lianne says, almost laughing. The family who used to live here left some photos behind by mistake. It's not a big deal.

She joins me at the table. We look down at the three photographs, which I have arranged in a row: the husband, the wife, the daughter. From upstairs, there is the sound of furniture being dragged around: Rhiannon reconfiguring her room again.

They all seem so sad, Lianne says.

She rests her head against my shoulder. I stare at the photographs. The daughter has her hair tied up in a bun, a little messy. I bend down to inspect the image.

What is it? Lianne asks.

I think she's wearing mascara, I say, although it's hard to tell for sure.

So?

Lianne's question hangs in the air as I inspect the photograph. I don't have an answer. I don't know why it matters. I only know that it does.

WE ARE in our bedroom in the dark and Lianne is on top of me and she's breathing and whispering in my ear, saying things. I'm holding her and there are moments when it doesn't feel like her at all, but someone else. I find myself imagining she is a woman who is like her but is not her, who looks a little different, who talks slightly differently, a woman more relaxed with less pretence, less brittle in manner, and I don't know why I'm thinking any of this, but the idea persists. It persists until I am imagining the woman in the photograph, her body in the dark moving against mine. Lianne's whispering in my ear and biting my neck and when she whispers *Derek* the thought comes suddenly, shockingly, that I'm not who she thinks I am. Don't call me that, I say. What do you want me to call you, she breathes, tell me what to call you. But I don't have an answer so I suddenly, roughly roll us over so that I am on top and in the darkness all I see beneath me is the woman from the photograph and she's gasping and now she's whispering what's got into you, what's got into you?

~

I CANNOT SLEEP. Downstairs, in the study, I go through the desk drawers until I find the file with our important paperwork. I sit down at the desk and in the yellow light of the lamp I flick through until I arrive at our birth certificates. The names are correct, and it is only then that I realise I had thought they could be wrong.

Unmoored again. A feeling like fight-or-flight. On the cusp of something but not knowing what.

At the back of the file is a plastic envelope containing our passports. Again, the names are right. But the man in the passport photograph that should be me is, instead, almost me. Not like a sibling or relation. Closer than that. Another kind of me. I go to the kitchen and come back with the photographs we've found. I place the one of the man next to the passport photo. They're the same person, although the version in the passport looks slightly younger.

What are you doing? Rhiannon is in the doorway, in her dressing gown. The yellow lamplight makes her seem jaundiced. Her shadow, thrown up against the far wall, is overgrown, warped.

I close the file.

Couldn't sleep, I say.

But what are you doing?

She takes a step into the room. I open the drawer to put the file away.

Just some paperwork, I tell her. House stuff.

She takes another step forward. Why are you lying?

I'm not lying, I reply, smiling.

Another silence. Rhiannon, watching me until I have to break the quiet: what?

Are you okay? she asks.

I'm fine.

You're always lying, she says.

She turns and walks out of the room. I put the file in the drawer and get up and follow her out. She's going up the stairs by the time I reach her.

Why are you up? I ask, keeping my voice low.

Couldn't sleep, she says.

We watch each other. The clock in the hallway ticks. I'm thinking about the birth certificates and the passports and the photographs inside them, and how I'm not thinking that those photographs are *wrong*, only that they are not what I expected. I'm trying to understand this, trying to parse what it might mean, and I'm thinking about the photographs we both found, me and this girl on the stairs who seems, suddenly, like a stranger, or rather someone I knew a long time ago but from whom I have grown estranged, and how the photographs we found and the photographs in the passports are of the same people, people who seem familiar, familiar yet strange, like this girl, my daughter, on the stairs.

Do you ever feel like you're really someone else? I ask her.

Her impassive stare becomes a frown. There is a glimmer of something—doubt, perhaps—but then it's gone.

No, she says. She looks past me to the clock on the wall. It's late, she says. I have school tomorrow. Then she turns and continues up into the dark, leaving me with the ticking clock and the yellowish light from the study.

In the dream they are both standing in the kitchen, the evening sun casting them in amber light. I am walking towards them. They are smiling. I reach out, my fingers splayed, and I touch their faces. Carefully, I work my fingertips behind their eyelids. Gently, I hook my thumbs inside their mouths. They let me do this. They smile around my fingers and thumbs as I begin to pull. To tear. The skin is like rubber, stretching, stretching, breaking apart, as I excavate to expose what lies beneath.

I wake up. Lianne is propped up on one elbow, saying my name, asking what's wrong. Behind her, the bedroom window is the deep indigo of first light.

You were talking, she whispers.

What was I saying?

It doesn't matter, she says, rubbing my chest, slow circles, trying to soothe me.

Tell me.

It doesn't matter, she says again.

Tell me.

Her hand stops moving across my chest. The shape of her beside me, looking down, featureless in the dark.

Photos, she says. You kept saying *photos*, over and over.

I breathe out. Close my eyes. Lianne lies down again. I stare at the ceiling, the faint slanted squares of light cast by the window. I consider getting up rather than trying to sleep again. I could go for a walk. I could go into the office early, get a head a start. I realise I'm looking for a reason not to be in this house.

I'm worried about you, Lianne says eventually.

Neither of us speak for a long time. The light in the window grows stronger. I assume Lianne is asleep until she asks, quietly, carefully, why I can't just be happy.

~

I'M DRIVING to work when the thought comes to me suddenly, like the blare of a horn: there are more photographs.

~

I LOCK my office door and go to my desk. Beyond the frosted glass, coworkers chat and drink coffee next to the photocopier. A telephone is ringing and no one is answering. It's nearly nine o'clock and I have a meeting to attend in the conference room in relation to cuts we need to make, the redundancies it will fall to me to announce.

The drawers in my desk are lockable, and I keep them locked. The key for the lock is very small and I keep it in my work satchel. This the only copy of the key. There is no duplicate.

When I arrived at work, when I was walking to the entrance, when I crossed the tiled foyer and got into the lift, there was a nagging feeling. A feeling that said: check the desk.

In the first drawer, under some paperwork and a cardboard folder, are three photographs. One shows the man. The other shows the woman. And finally there is the daughter.

The photographs are all polaroids. The man took his own

picture, judging from the angle. He looks worried. The pictures of the woman and the girl have a similar quality, an air of fear, although they were not the photographers. The photographs were all taken in the same room: the kitchen of our house.

A telephone is still ringing and no one is answering. My colleagues are gone from their spot at the photocopier.

The telephone is the one on my desk. I pick up.

Are you coming to this meeting or not? a voice says on the line.

Yes, I respond. Yes. I'll be there now.

AFTER THE MEETING I grab one of the interns by her arm. She startles at first but as she turns and sees that it's me, one of the bosses, her face transforms into a practiced smile. I let go of her arm. I smile back. I tell her I want her opinion about something. I ask her if she thinks I've changed at all. The intern—Lucy—she keeps smiling and, after the briefest pause, gives a small laugh. Is there anything different about me? I ask. Her smile remains but there's a hint of confusion now, like this is a trick question. Like she doesn't know how best to answer. Eventually, when it's gone on too long, I tell her never mind, she can go, and she goes out on to the main office floor, and for a while I stand alone in the conference room looking out of the wide windows at the city centre rooftops.

LEAVING WORK, I can only think of the photographs in the drawer. I know the answer but I spiral around it like water swirling around a black drain.

I find myself driving a different route, a longer route, back to the house. *The house.* When did I stop thinking of it as home? I take the A-road rather than the motorway. Soon after, I turn off the A-road and drive through town, then the side streets. The drawers in my office are always locked and only I have the key. I drive through terraced streets, rows of old brick houses with small dark windows and sagging slate roofs, many converted into maisonettes, bedsits, student housing. I remember living in a place like this, although I haven't thought about it for years. A draughty rental. A landlord who refused to fix the kitchen's leaking flat roof, a brown stain spreading across the ceiling like a filthy cloud. The drawers are kept locked and only I have the key. I keep driving. It starts to rain. The suburbs, now, a little more space between the houses. All of it new-build estates, knotted rabbit-warren streets and closes, rises and cul-de-sacs, where every house looks the same. So easy to lose yourself inside. We lived here, once, I think —a starter home, cheaply built, walls like cardboard—we *must* have, but where is the memory, the actual memory, rather than a vague feeling? And beyond all of this, after a while: the older suburbs, the grand 1930s detached houses, imposing behind their generous front gardens, their manicured lawns, their BMWs and Audis and Jaguars lying idle on gravel or blockwork driveways, fringed with clipped hydrangeas and pruned privet hedges, all watched over by dormer loft conversions and fresh paint and wooden shutter-blinds and there, finally, its windows dim, its gravel driveway wide and empty like an open, hungry mouth: our house.

We didn't always live here, I think.

The drawers in my office are locked and only I have the key.

We didn't used to be like this.

Me, standing in gloom, speaking to my daughter on the stairs: Do you ever feel like you're really someone else?

WHEN LIANNE ARRIVES home there is a brief silence. Then she begins to shout my name. The longer I take to answer, the more panicked she sounds. This is understandable; I've made a mess of the house, opening cupboards, emptying them, upending boxes, pulling out drawers. It looks like we have been burgled.

There are so many photographs.

She finds me in one of the spare bedrooms. I'm on my knees, prizing up the carpet beneath the large bay window with my fingertips. I keep catching my nails. I should get a flathead screwdriver from the garage.

What are you doing? she says from the doorway, eyes wide.

I'm finding more photographs, I reply, returning my attention to the carpet. I've found seventeen more.

Please, Derek, you'll ruin the carpet, it won't go back down the same —

I think there's another one under here.

Why?

Because I remember. Or I think I remember. Vaguely.

I don't understand, Lianne says. What do you remember?

I finally stop what I'm doing and still on my knees I turn around and look at her. *I did it,* I say, smiling. *I took the photos. I hid them,* a long time ago, when we were different.

I need to show her. I go to the garage and come back with the largest flathead screwdriver I can find and a hammer. I crouch beside the skirting board in our bedroom and work the head of the screwdriver in at the top, working the metal between the skirting board and the wall. I tap the handle with the hammer and begin to prize the board away. The wood splits. Lianne is shouting at me. I tell her it's fine, we can repair it, it's not like we don't have the money. Stop, Lianne is saying, just stop. Rhiannon is in the doorway asking what's going on and Lianne shouts for her to go to her room but I'm not paying any attention, because I've pulled the skirting board away from the wall now, and behind it, having waited in the tight dusty dark for this very moment, are dozens of photographs. They fall outward, scattering on to the carpet, and I gather several up and offer them to Lianne as though they are a precious treasure. See? I'm saying, grinning. See? It's us. I took the photos, I hid them so we'd remember one day. We didn't always used to be like this, did we? We were other people, once—

Shut up, Lianne says.

Something in her face. In the way she has forced all expression away. In the way she holds her mouth, the thin line of it, the way she isn't blinking, the way she's looking down at me.

Shut up, she says.

Do you remember? I ask, gazing up.

You're scaring me, she says quietly.

∿

WE ARGUE. Lianne gets upset. She tells me I'm making her feel unsafe. She tells me to stop talking.

I sleep downstairs in the lounge, on the sofa, curling myself like a foetus under the Kashmir throw. I feel like I should cry but I can't. This strange feeling: cleaned out, hollowed out. Like a weight has lifted, a weight I didn't know was there until I suddenly did, and by seeing it, by speaking it—we were not always like this, we changed, and we forgot—

Lianne stands in the lounge doorway. A shape in the dark. Her hands rise to her face. She rubs her eyes. I wait for her to say something.

I'm worried, Derek. I think you're having an episode.

Is Rhiannon awake? I ask.

Don't you dare talk to her about this.

She watches me for a moment, then turns and goes away. I listen to her going up the stairs. I roll over and press my face into the sofa cushions, the deeper darkness.

I WAKE up and Rhiannon is standing at the end of the sofa. There is a gap in the curtains of the bay window, and a strip of morning light runs down the middle of her, bisecting her.

Hey, she says softly.

It wasn't a dream, I say eventually.

What wasn't?

When I saw my reflection. When I saw the other reflection.

Rhiannon doesn't answer. Upstairs, there are footsteps, the bathroom door closing. Lianne hasn't slept well, either.

Do you remember who we used to be? I ask quietly. Do you remember the other Rhiannon?

I don't know who that is, she says. But I've always been here, Dad.

I get up from the sofa. She shrinks backwards, towards the door. I tell her to follow me. When she refuses, I take her by the hand and I lead her into the study, to the desk. Look at these, I'm saying as I pull open the desk drawers, as I'm lifting the file and placing it down on the desk.

Look at what? she says.

I open the file to the plastic envelopes where our passports are kept.

Look at what? she says again.

The plastic envelopes are empty.

Where are they? I'm saying.

Where are what?

We didn't used to be like this, I'm muttering, flicking through the file, checking between each page, rummaging through the drawers. We didn't used to *be* like this.

Why are you talking like that? Rhiannon says. Talk properly.

It's just how I talk, I reply.

No it's not, she says. You're talking like some council estate –

And then Lianne is there, having come downstairs, having found me in the study, at the desk, with our daughter, when Lianne had told me not to involve her, because apparently I'm frightening, apparently I'm scaring them both. Lianne is there, and she's shouting, she's pulling Rhiannon away, pushing her out of the room. Lianne is shouting at me, what is wrong with you, what is *wrong* with you, and I'm shouting back, finally, and I'm saying where are they, what have you done with them, and Lianne says what are you talking about and I say our old faces, our fucking *faces*.

I'M AWAY from the house for a while after that. Some weeks. I have to be away for a while because Lianne calls our doctor. At first I think I might change again, might change back, gradually. Each morning I look in the mirror, inspecting, searching for subtle differences. Lianne visits, but not Rhiannon, who is too upset according to Lianne. In the sessions they tell me it's okay. They tell me that everyone changes gradually, over time. Sometimes they ask if I think the house did it—changed us, that is—because apparently I hinted to them, early on, that I thought this was the case. I tell them no. And this is true—I don't know how it happened. I only know that it did.

The trick, I eventually learn, is to echo.

People change, I start saying. It's normal. I shrug and throw up my hands as though I'm simply embarrassed about the whole episode.

Rhiannon starts coming to the hospital with Lianne. So as not to scare her away again, I pretend that there's nothing different about her or her mother.

Soon I am discharged.

The medication doesn't alter what I think. It just makes me not care as much.

IN THE DREAM they are standing in the kitchen, the evening sun casting them in amber light. I am walking towards them and they are smiling. I reach out, fingers spread wide, and I touch their faces. With great care, I work my fingertips behind their eyelids. I hook my thumbs into their mouths. They allow this, smiling around my fingers and thumbs as I begin, slowly, to pull. Their faces stretch, then tear. There is blood but not as much as there ought to be. I pull the flesh away and I wipe away the blood and I am sure that underneath it all are my wife and my daughter, their real selves, their selves which are more them than what they are now, in a way that I cannot put into words. But as I wipe away the ragged ribbons of flesh and blood, all that's there to greet me are the same faces, the same thems. I begin to make a noise, and the noise is laughter. Because they are the same. It's all they are now, all the way down, all the way in. And they are smiling still, this woman and this girl who are, just slightly, maddeningly, strange to me. And now they are reaching towards my face. They are hooking their fingers into my mouth, my nostrils, the corners of my eyes.

When I wake up in the dark next to this woman who is not really my wife, in this house I do not really belong in, I am laughing.

Tearful, I am laughing at the ceiling. The sound bounces off the tastefully decorated walls, the faintest echo, the slightest doubling. Laughing, laughing. Until the laughter no longer sounds like my own. Until it seems, almost, to belong to someone else entirely.

Contributors

David Demchuk's third novel *The Butcher's Daughter*, co-written with debut author Corinne Leigh Clark, was published this May by Soho Press (US) and Titan Books (UK). Born and raised on the Canadian prairie, David lives by the sea with his husband in St. John's, Newfoundland.

Orrin Grey is a Rondo Award-nominated writer, editor, and film scholar, as well as the author of several spooky books. His stories of ghosts, monsters, and sometimes the ghosts of monsters can be found in dozens of anthologies, including Ellen Datlow's *Best Horror of the Year*. He resides in the suburbs of Kansas City, where he watches lots of scary movies. You can visit him online at orringrey.com.

Vince Haig is an illustrator, designer, and author. You can visit Vince at his website: barquing.com

This is **Andrew Humphrey's** second appearance in *Weird Horror*. He has also been published in many other magazines, such as *Black Static*, *The Third Alternative*, *Crimewave*, *Bare Bone*, and *Midnight Street*. His collection, *Other Voices*, was a winner of the inaugural East Anglian Book Awards. He has had two other collections published, along with two novels. He lives and works in Norwich, in the U.K.

Cyan Katz is a criminal QTPOC elder living in Berlin, Germany. A punk bodhisattva still filled with wanderlust after all these years, they've been previously published in the dark fiction anthology, *120 Murders*. They're preoccupied with transformation, body-centrism, and the care and feeding of monsters in our universal oceans. You can visit them at TheIlluminatedBody.com Instagram @the_illuminated_body, or Bluesky @CyanKatz

Jack Klausner lives in the U.K. This is his second appearance in *Weird Horror*. His short fiction has also appeared in *The Dark, ergot, Fictionable,* and elsewhere. You can find him at jackklausner.com or on Bluesky @jackklausner

Mary Kuryla's collection *Freak Weather Stories* (University of Massachusetts Press) received the Grace Paley Prize in Short Fiction. Her stories have appeared in *The Paris Review, Conjunctions, The Baffler, Strange Horizons, Cosmic Horror Monthly*, and elsewhere and have received The Pushcart Prize. Her novel *Away to Stay* (Regal House Publishing) was called "a delightfully quirky debut" by *Publishers Weekly*. Kuryla's award-winning shorts and feature film have premiered at Sundance and Toronto. She is a screenwriting and horror film professor in the School of Film and TV at Loyola Marymount University.

Valin Mattheis is a self-taught artist from California, now residing in France. His work concerns subjects of awe and dread, the monstrous and the sublime. When he isn't hunched over his desk, bleary eyed with brush in hand, he attempts to write. Find him at Strange-gods.com Instagram @strangegodsart

David Peak's most recent book is *The World Below* (Apocalypse Party). He lives in Chicago.

Rory Say is a Canadian writer from Victoria, BC, whose work tends toward the dark and the strange. Stories of his have recently appeared in *The New Quarterly, Metastellar, Uncharted,* the *Northern*

Nights anthology, and previously in *Weird Horror*. A mini-collection, titled *Different Faces*, was published last year by Dim Shores, while a full-length collection, *My Secrets Are of the Grave*, is forthcoming via Lethe Press. Read more by visiting his website: rorysay.com

Simon Strantzas is the author of several collections of short fiction, including *Other Sides* (Lethe Press, 2025), and editor of a number of anthologies, including *Year's Best Weird Fiction, Vol. 3*. Combined, he's been a finalist for four Shirley Jackson Awards, two British Fantasy Awards, and the World Fantasy Award. His fiction has appeared in numerous annual best-of anthologies, and in venues such as *Nightmare*, *The Dark*, and *Cemetery Dance*. In 2014, his edited anthology, *Aickman's Heirs*, won the Shirley Jackson Award. He lives with his wife in Toronto, Canada. Visit him at strantzas.com

Jocelyn Szczepaniak-Gillece teaches Film Studies at the University of Wisconsin-Milwaukee; her weird fiction appears or will appear in places like *Apocalypse Confidential, Exacting Clam, Sublunary Review, The Quarter(ly)*, and others. Her first novel, *Poltergeist*, is forthcoming with Apocalypse Confidential.

Juniper White (she/her) is a red fox, a librarian, and a ghost haunting a house in Portland, OR. She is a trans author of Palestinian descent. Find her stories in *Apex Magazine, hex literary, Crow & Cross Keys*, and more; find her on Bluesky @JuneWhiteWrites. If she was a plant, she'd be a wisteria.

A.C. Wise is the author of the novels *Wendy, Darling, Hooked*, and *The Ballad of the Bone Road* (forthcoming January 2026), along with the short story collection, *The Ghost Sequences*, among other titles. Her work has won the Sunburst Award, and been a finalist for the Nebula, World Fantasy, Stoker, Locus, British Fantasy, Aurora, Shirley Jackson, Ignyte, and Lambda Literary Awards. In addition to her fiction, she contributes regular review columns to *Locus* and *Apex Magazine*. More info at www.acwise.net.

www.ingramcontent.com/pod-product-compliance
Lightning Source LLC
LaVergne TN
LVHW090607010725
815070LV00001B/25